The
Yearbook

CAROL MASCIOLA

MeritPress

To Ibon, Endika, and Leonardo

Published by
Merit Press
an imprint of F+W Media, Inc.
10151 Carver Road, Suite 200
Blue Ash, OH 45242. U.S.A.
www.meritpressbooks.com

ISBN 10: 1-4405-8897-X
ISBN 13: 978-1-4405-8897-6
eISBN 10: 1-4405-8898-8
eISBN 13: 978-1-4405-8898-3

Printed in the United States of America.

10 9 8 7 6 5 4 3 2 1

Library of Congress Cataloging-in-Publication Data

Masciola, Carol.
  The yearbook / Carol Masciola.
    pages cm
  ISBN 978-1-4405-8897-6 (hc) -- ISBN 1-4405-8897-X (hc) -- ISBN 978-1-4405-8898-3 (ebook) -- ISBN 1-4405-8898-8 (ebook)
  [1. Time travel--Fiction. 2. Love--Fiction. 3. High schools--Fiction. 4. Schools--Fiction. 5. Mental illness--Fiction.] I. Title.
  PZ7.1.V55Ye 2015
  [Fic]--dc23
                            2015012375

Cover design by Christina Riddle and Frank Rivera.
Cover image © hello-tuesday.deviantart.com.

This book is available at quantity discounts for bulk purchases.
For information, please call 1-800-289-0963.

Acknowledgments

Special thanks to my editor, Jacquelyn Mitchard, to my agents Jacqueline Flynn and Joelle Delbourgo and their intern Sammy Brown, to Christina Riddle of Edgewater Graphics for her cover and to Frank Rivera for his contributions to the design, to Katie McDonough for her careful copyediting, and to Claudia Schou of the Media Boutique in Long Beach, California, for advising me on my book query.

One

Lola glanced over her shoulder. The man in the turtleneck sweater was still following her. She didn't know who he was or what he wanted, but there was no doubt he had called her name and chased her when she fled.

She turned down the east corridor and ran for the restroom. An *OUT OF ORDER* sign was taped over the *GIRLS* sign. She kicked the locked door and looked around for another hiding place. In a few long strides she was inside the library, the door hissing shut behind her.

"You're late," said a voice, and a husky woman in a Cleveland Browns sweatshirt and Lycra jeans emerged from behind a bookshelf. She frowned at her wristwatch. "Or else you're early. Anyhow, you're not on time."

"For what?" Lola said.

"Aren't you my little helper from the detention hall?"

Lola thought of the man in the turtleneck. He didn't look like campus security. Probation, maybe? Social Services? By now he was probably lurking just outside the library door, trying to pick up her trail. "Yeah. I guess I'm the helper," she said.

"Good. Come with me. We had a little incident that requires some janitorial activity."

The woman moved into the stacks and Lola followed. She had been in the library a few times but had never noticed the low door at the back of the room. She was glad to see the work would take place out of plain view. The woman turned a rusty key in the lock and the door groaned open.

"Here's the reserve room. Or, as I've come to think of it, *the refuse room.*" She snorted at her own joke.

Lola looked around. It was one of the most impressive messes she'd ever seen, and as a part-time employee of an unsanitary chicken restaurant, she'd seen plenty. The tiny room was scorched but also soggy, as if it had been both set on fire and flooded. Books and parts of books were strewn about like the debris that washes up on the beach after a storm.

"How did *this* happen?" she asked.

"It caught fire, then the sprinklers came on."

"And what am I supposed to do?"

"Just start chucking every ' 'ng into that garbage bin. If you want I can try to get you the   ow shovel, but it might take a while. I gotta fill out a form."

The woman handed Lola a pa   of rubber gloves and turned back in the direction of her desk. Lc   inspected the shelves. They were jam-packed and sour with mild   She climbed onto a table and opened the window. The morning   rizzle had stopped, and a breeze entered on a shaft of sunlight. Th.   vas better. Lola jumped back down and called out the door, "Hel.   Library lady?"

"Mrs. Dubois. Whaddaya want?"

"I'll need a stool to reach those top shelves, or a ladder, even."

"Forget it," Mrs. Dubois yelled back. "Safety regulations don't allow students to be climbing up on ladders and breaking their necks. Just stand on that table. But it wobbles. Don't break your neck. And shut the door. That stink is killing me."

Lola shut the door. The odor was tolerable now with the window open. She took off her knapsack and placed it on the table, angling it to cover the spot where someone had scratched *YOU SUCK* into the Formica. She snapped on the gloves.

Most of the books on the lower shelves were beyond saving, and beyond Lola: heavy volumes full of chemical symbols that fell to pieces at her touch, leather-bound sets on local history, now bloated and squishy. Lola tossed *The Natural History of Ashfield County, Ohio, Through 1900* into the bin, thinking how it had lasted so long only to meet the same fate as today's banana peels and pencil shavings and snotty Kleenexes. She skimmed the sticky pages of *The Temperance Lesson Book: Short Lessons on Alcohol and Its Action on the Body*, 1878 edition, and sent it flapping after its ill-fated predecessors. She was about to do likewise to *Stories of Ohio*, by a certain William Dean Howells, when, before she knew it, she was on page 36:

In his old age Logan wandered from place to place, broken by the misfortunes of his people, and homeless in his own land. He fell prey to drink, and was at last murdered near Detroit, where, as the story goes, he was sitting by his campfire, and lost in gloomy thought, when an Indian whom he had offended stole upon him and sank his tomahawk into—

"What are you doing?" It was Mrs. Dubois, evidently back from lunch, filling the doorway.

"Reading," Lola said.

"Don't read. Throw."

Lola sat up and stretched. "How'd this fire start?"

Mrs. Dubois picked thoughtfully at the space between her front teeth with a bejeweled thumbnail. "It's the damnedest thing. They don't know. The fire people, they've been all over it with their detective kit. Just poof. It was on fire."

Mrs. Dubois left at two o'clock, threatening to return in an hour to check Lola's progress, but she didn't come back. Without anyone to tell her not to read the doomed books, she sat down on the squeaky folding chair next to the table and continued as the light from the window faded. Other notable books came and went. There were covers without pages, and pages without covers. *The Ashfield County Herbarium* had shed its pressed bluebells and wood lilies and expired in the muck. Lola wondered if any of the seeds would sprout in the dump, and then if anybody would pick the flowers and press them in a book, and then if the book would end up in a flooded library, and then—she realized she was hungry. She launched *The Ashfield County Herbarium* toward the bin and went prowling for food.

She bought a bag of Doritos from the snack machine next to the gym, noticing with irritation that they were expired, and climbed into a far corner of the bleachers to eat them. Down below, a bunch of student council doofs were decorating the place for that night's dance. They'd managed to get the disco ball to rotate, but feedback from the speakers could have withered eardrums halfway down the block. Lola followed the rotations of the disco ball, and her mind began to wander. She was thinking how strange it was to be back in Ashfield. She had been away ten years, not far away, still in the same county, but during all that time Ashfield had been like a hazy dream place to her, not a real place you could get to in a car. Yet here she was. Lots of people still recognized her name, and remembered certain things about her that she wished they didn't.

Lola had gone to several schools and had not done well at any of them. The last had expelled her for chronic truancy and poor academic performance. She had been failing every class. Mrs. Hershey, Lola's social worker, had talked to her in a new, ominous way that made her hide under the bedcovers. Most of the speech was forgotten, locked away in the vault of unbearable things, but a few choice lines still rang in Lola's ears, especially at night: *You have to pass these classes. What will you do in life without a high school diploma? It's almost too late.*

The memory intruded now, and she took off her lucky baseball cap and swatted at the air, as if the words were swarming around her head. She knew it was a funny, not-quite-right thing to do, but it made her feel better. She was still swatting when she noticed half a dozen cheerleaders watching her from the gym floor. One of them whispered something to the others, and then Lola saw them snicker.

"What's funny, morons?" she called down, which startled them nicely. She hated to be noticed, to be observed. It was all right if it was only the other freaks from the group home looking. But the stares of regular kids, normal kids, seemed to shrink her, to make her feel like something you'd step over on the street.

She stomped down the bleachers and back toward the cozy safety of the library. She knew she was expected at the group home for dinner. She hadn't asked for a pass. But she pushed that thought from her mind, back into the crawlspace with her stacks of unfinished homework, the snickers in the gym, the stranger in the turtleneck sweater.

The reserve room was dark now. She snapped on the lights and a fluorescent tube flickered on overhead, lending a sickly yellow-green glow to the disaster area. She climbed up onto the tricky table again and examined one of the high shelves. With a screech, the solid place where she had been leaning her left hand gave way like a door opening up, revealing a dark nook in the shelf. Lola peeked into the space, fearing spiders or a mouse skeleton, and after a moment worked up the courage to put her hand inside and feel around. She pulled out a Mercury head dime dated 1920, an old pack of matches, an empty glass bottle, and a yellowed business card. Lola read the card: *Downing's Millinery Shop: Evening and Daywear for Fashionable Ladies and Girls, 2112 Main Street, Ashfield.* She pocketed the dime and the business card, making a mental note to look up *millinery* in the dictionary someday, and tossed the rest into the trash. Then she wiped off her dusty hands on her jeans and began to clear the next shelf.

Taking out the first few books, she found another row hidden behind, perfectly dry. Like gallant soldiers, the books in the first rank had sacrificed themselves to save those in the second. Lola pulled out the first dry book she touched; *ASHFIELD HIGH: 1924*, it said. It was an old yearbook.

Lola jumped off the table and sat down to leaf through it. The brittle pages gave off a pleasant smell, like smoky acorns. Near the front was a full-page picture of Ashfield High School. Could this be the same ratty building in which she now sat? Yes, the front was recognizable, with its pillars and gargoyles. Clean and new, without the graffiti, Ashfield High looked to Lola like a courthouse or a museum. The shabby portable classrooms that leeched onto both wings were missing. The school sat on a wide lawn instead of its sheet of cracked and weedy cement. The mermaid fountain looked new and pretty. Lola wondered when the poor mermaid had been decapitated, and by what idiot.

She turned the page and the ghosts of Ashfield High began to appear. The young, serious faces looked back at her from their faded oval portraits. Lola was caught off-guard by a tight yearning in her chest that she didn't understand. *This one I'll keep*, she thought, and slipped the book into her knapsack. She rested her head on the thin canvas of the bag, and her drowsy brain shuffled the scraps she'd read from a hundred different books that day, trying to organize them into a story. The Friday night dance had begun in the gym, and the distant thump of the bass echoed down the hallway. *Gaga Oo-la-la*. Soon she was asleep.

TWO

The scrape of chair legs woke her sometime later. She lifted her head to see a young woman dragging a wooden stool across the floor. The light was dim, as if the electricity was at half power. Giggling to herself, the woman climbed the stool and reached for the top shelf. The hidden compartment reappeared from behind the trick board, and she drew out the glass bottle. She took a sip, shuddered, and smacked her lips.

That old bottle was empty, Lola thought. *And besides, I'm sure I threw it away.* "Nightcap?" Lola said.

The woman whirled around on the stool and seemed startled to see Lola sitting there. "Shhh," she hissed.

Lola saw then that the woman was really a teenager in some kind of freak costume. A silky pink dress fell to her shins, and a whole lot of tinkling glass beads swung along her front. She wore a bell-shaped hat with a feathery brim, long white gloves, and chunky heels, white with big silver buckles.

Lola stared at the weird shoes on the heavy wooden stool. Where had that stool been all day while she was risking her neck on that wobbly Formica table? And where, by the way, was the wobbly table? Because Lola was now seated at a wide oak desk. *This is not the room where I fell asleep*, Lola thought. *Did I sleepwalk here?* She looked around more carefully. *No, it is the same room. I'm sure it is. But the room has changed.* The big rubber garbage bin was gone from its place in the corner, as was all evidence of fire and flood. The stench of mold and ashes had been replaced by the pleasant, papery scent of a library. A leather sofa stretched against one wall, with goose-necked reading lamps positioned on tables at each end. The books glowed in that strange half-light. Who had cleaned the room? How? And when? Under her baseball cap, her scalp prickled.

The girl in pink took another nip and jumped down from her perch.

"Hey," Lola said. "Where's the stuff that was here? Wait a minute."

But in a swish of silk she was gone.

Lola scrambled up from the desk and chased the girl along the wide, echoing halls of Ashfield High. The floors were glossy as pools in moonlight, as if they'd just been waxed. The music from the Friday night dance grew louder but was nothing like the pounding pop that had lulled her to sleep. It sounded curiously like a live orchestra playing bouncy cartoon music.

The girl in pink vanished into the gym. Lola was stopped in the doorway by a sight that hit her like a punch in the face. The gym was a mass of color and motion, like a flower garden in a storm. Thunder seemed to rise up out of the floor as the dancers' hard heels struck the wooden planks. The girls were dressed like the one in the library, some with added sequins and feathers, and most with white gloves that stretched past their elbows. The boys wore scratchy-looking suits and neckties and moved with a kind of elastic joy. Something was radically wrong. Not just in the library, but here, too.

Lola stepped warily into the gym. A twenty-piece orchestra was playing on the stage, and a man sang through his nose: *"Every morning, every evening, ain't we got fun?"* In a state of tremendous confusion, Lola sidled along the wall. *"Not much money, oh, but honey, ain't we got fun?"* the man went on, as Lola came up alongside the refreshment table. The girl in pink was a few feet away. She stood in front of an immense crystal bowl of bright red punch, pouring booze into it from the bottle she held behind her back.

"Hey, you," Lola called.

The girl looked up. "Moi?"

"What is all this?" Lola said. Her sudden idea was that the gym had been rented out for a music video or a movie scene. What was this supposed to be, the 40s? The 50s? The olden days, anyway. She looked around for cameras but couldn't see through the crowd.

"You're not from the Temperance League, are you, little man?" the girl answered. "Let me assure you, sir, that this bottle contains nothing but the purest lemonade."

Sir? Lola turned and looked behind her. Was this girl talking to *her*? Was she blind?

"You wanna dance with me, right? You wanna dance with me, but you're shy," the girl went on. She had skipped over to Lola and was yanking her by the arm. "I'm Whoopsie."

"What?" Lola shouted over the music.

"Whoopsie Whipple. I don't recognize you, shorty. You're sure a little guy. But I don't mind. I was a late bloomer myself. Didn't get my first powder puff till last year."

"You need glasses," Lola said.

But Whoopsie didn't seem to hear. She just kept dragging Lola by the sleeve of her sweatshirt, deeper into the throbbing, thrashing heart of the dance. Lola had failed so far to see any cameras. It was as if she had wandered straight into the past. She felt like crying, or laughing, or running. She hoped some explanation would present itself before she fainted.

"You dance funny," Whoopsie said.

"We have different dances where I come from," Lola said.

"Oh yeah? Where's that?"

"New York," Lola said. She sometimes lied when she felt stressed. She heard the words coming out of her mouth but had a sense that she wasn't completely in control of them.

"Really and truly? A real, live New Yorker. You're the first one I ever met," Whoopsie said. "I'm going to New York someday. I'm gonna shake the dust of this hick town off my heels and make a name for myself."

Lola watched the girl's face as she talked. It wasn't a strange face—just the face of another human being, with eyes, a nose, and a mouth with slightly oversized teeth. Maybe if she focused on these small, normal things, she could keep the panic away until she figured out what was going on here.

"Tell me all about New York," Whoopsie said.

"Well, it's very big," Lola said. "And crowded, and—"

"Confidentially, I, myself, will be seeing the Big Apple soon, sooner than anybody in this hick town could ever conceive of," Whoopsie said. "I've entered a magazine contest, see, to be a real, live chorus girl on the Broadway stage. All I had to do was send in my photograph and measurements. You can't tell anybody, though. Nobody around here has a lick of ambition. The day I get my acceptance telegram, I'll wave it in Mother and Daddy's faces and then they'll fall right over in a dead faint. They don't have a lick of ambition, either."

"You're an actress, then, right?" Lola said. "And all of this is—?"

"I've always been an actress at heart," Whoopsie said. She plucked at Lola's sleeve. "I never saw a pullover with words on it before. Nike? Is that your name? Shouldn't it say, 'Mike'? Is it a misprint, Mike?"

"It's a shoe company," Lola said as they moved past the orchestra, but her words were lost in the high note of a clarinet.

"Come on, Mike from New York. Dance over this way. I wanna make Thumbtack jealous."

Whoopsie Whipple's beads shook, whacking Lola in the face in time to the music, as they danced sideways toward a ferocious-looking person in a dark suit who was daintily drinking a cup of punch. Thumbtack's hair was slicked down and parted in the middle, and a tiny bowtie rode high on his white collar. Lola saw him deposit his cup on a table and start toward them.

"You New Yorkers certainly can cut a rug, Mike," Whoopsie shouted at Lola when she was sure Thumbtack was close enough to hear. "I don't know if I'm ready for a steady beau, but I'll certainly consider your appealing offer."

Thumbtack's big hand clamped down on Lola's shoulder, and he glared down at the top of her baseball cap. "Hey, farmer," he said. "Keep your paws off my gal."

I'm having a nightmare, that's all, Lola decided as the big man squeezed her collarbone. *It's from eating those expired Doritos. They don't put that expiration date on there for nothing.*

"Thumbtack Matthews, for the love of cucumbers," Whoopsie said.

"Keep 'em off, hayseed, or it's knuckle-sandwich time," Thumbtack growled. He gave Lola a shove. She stumbled backward a step, then rebounded and kicked him hard in the shin of his tweed pants.

"Ow. Why, you!" he yelled. "All right, you asked for it."

Whoopsie screamed and Thumbtack charged, nostrils flaring, like a bull in the cartoons. Lola fled into the cyclone of heels and elbows. *"Yes sir, that's my baby,"* someone was singing in a high tenor. *"No sir, don't mean maybe."* And then, there it was: the exit. *I've got to get out of this gym,* she thought. *If I can get out of this gym, maybe I'll wake up.* She skirted the refreshment table and was almost free when she slipped on a pile of peanut shells and went into a long skid. Then she was down on the floor, Thumbtack glowering over her with clenched fists as the dance raged on around them. She shut her eyes.

"Matthews, you ugly mug. Why don't you let the little fellow be?" someone said.

Lola opened her eyes. A man in a suit and tie—no, a teenager in a man's suit and tie—had stepped out of the crowd and imposed himself between her and Thumbtack.

"Stay out of this, Hemmings," Thumbtack said.

"He's just a tiny little runt after all," the elegant young man in the suit said. He was shifting playfully from side to side, blocking and reblocking Thumbtack's access to the supposed farmer.

"You just go ahead on back to your laboratory, professor," Thumbtack said. "What made you decide to come to a dance?"

"I don't know. The mood struck me," Hemmings said. "Lucky for this little farmer, I'd say."

Down on the gym floor, Lola picked the peanut shells from her sweatshirt and watched the pair argue. Yes, it had to be the vivid edge of a dream, one of those high-definition experiences that can come right before waking, but of an intensity she never would have thought possible. She took off her baseball cap to swat the dream away, and everybody turned to gape at her. It wasn't the swatting they were looking at, she realized, but the long, thick ponytail that had tumbled from inside her cap.

Lola's defender put a hand to his heart. "Why, you're a girl!" He looked her up and down again. "Aren't you?"

Lola struggled to her feet. "Are you all blind? Is this a blind people's dance?" she shouted at the group, even though she'd just decided they were only dream characters. "Of course I'm a girl."

Thumbtack blushed to his hairline and hid his fists behind his back. "Golly ding. I've never seen a girl in waist overalls before. Do pardon me, miss." He made a slight bow and crunched away over the peanut shells. Whoopsie Whipple danced after him.

The young man who had protected Lola crouched down and scooped a broken necklace off the floor. "Is this yours?" he said. "Looks like somebody danced on it."

Lola nodded dismally. It was her favorite necklace, the initial *L* suspended from a silver chain. She had found it on a sidewalk when she was twelve. She liked to tell people it was an heirloom from an aunt or a grandmother, although she'd had neither.

"Busted chain, I'm afraid," he said, handing it back to her. "I could fix it for you. I've got a little workshop. Every kind of tool you can think of, and some I invented myself."

She stared at him. He was familiar somehow. She'd seen him somewhere—the strong jaw, the dark wavy chestnut hair—but then again, maybe not, because if she had, she certainly wouldn't have forgotten who he was. The dream softened and sweetened as she looked at him, and thoughts of fleeing the gym were replaced by thoughts of stretching out the experience. She extended the necklace to him. He closed his palm over it, and over Lola's entire hand as well, guiding her into the crowd of dancers. The orchestra had eased into a slow, dreamy number. In a moment she was in his arms, gliding along, or gliding as well as anybody can in thick basketball treads. The steps weren't too complicated, and before long she stopped watching the other girls' feet. He told her his name was Peter Hemmings, and then she introduced herself.

"See here, Miss Lundy, I'm sorry I thought you were a boy. I'm very stupid. Now that I've had a good look at you, I can plainly see you don't look at all like a boy, except for your—"

"You mean my costume?" Lola said. "I'm in this play, see, and we just had a performance. I play the role of a—"

"A hobo?" Peter guessed.

"How did you guess?" Lola said. "Yes, indeed. A hobo."

"But your shoes. I've never seen a hobo with shoes like that. I've never seen anyone with shoes like that."

"They're from France," Lola said. "Paris, France. My aunt sent them to me. Pretty soon everybody will have a pair."

"I don't doubt it. The girls around here are crazy for all that French stuff."

They danced along the south wall, past a row of chairs, and Lola discarded her cap. With a flick of the wrist, she released her hair from its rubber band and let it fall, sandy brown, past her shoulders. She wasn't going to be called "sir" again if she could help it.

Peter squeezed her hand. "I'd like to see that play of yours, Lola. I'll bet it's swell."

"Play?"

"About the hobo."

"I'm afraid tonight was our last performance." Lola snapped her fingers. "Too bad. It *was* swell."

"A play and a dance, and all in the same night," Peter said. "You're a social butterfly."

Lola smiled at him. What kind of eyes did he have, that he could see her that way? In her short life she'd collected a number of labels: socially awkward, socially unacceptable, social outcast, Social Services client. But social butterfly?

"I am fairly active socially," she said. "It's my nature."

The longer the dance went on, the harder it was for Lola to accept that she could be dreaming. The exertion had brought a mist of sweat to her forehead, and she keenly felt her heart beating, her lungs sucking in the perfumed air. She looked at Peter's hand in hers, at the blue veins just visible under his skin. Everything was utterly solid and consistent. She had never felt more awake.

"You've got me beat," Peter was saying. "I've been rather a hermit lately, holed up with my inventions." He whirled her in and out. *One-two-three-and-four. Five. Rotate. Seven-and-eight.*

"What do you invent?"

"Oh, all sorts of things. It's a hobby. I want to be a scientist."

"What kind of a scientist?"

"I want to disprove bunkum."

"What's that?"

"Séances, necromancy, fortune telling, spiritualism, all that."

Lola nodded. "Oh. You mean bull. Stuff that's a crock."

"No, no. This has nothing to do with cookery. What I mean is, people have no business clinging to Medieval superstitions in 1923. It's just willful ignorance to keep on turning away from what science has brought us and . . ." Peter kept talking, but Lola didn't hear the rest.

He said 1923. And I'm here. I am not in a dream. How did I get here? How many years ago? How many years ago? Ten, twenty, thirty, fifty. No. Start over. Subtract twenty, forty, seventy, eighty, ninety. I can't get it. I need a calculator.

"You're shivering," Peter said. "Is anything wrong?"

"No, no. Not shivering." *Should I say something? Alert somebody? Of course not. They'd have me hauled away in a straitjacket. And I wouldn't blame them.*

Peter put a hand on her shoulder. "You *are* shivering. They've got hot cider tonight. Come on. Let's have some."

Peter filled two cups with dark brown cider. Lola took a gulp and shuddered. Somebody had spiked the cider, too. The warmth flowed down into her insides and steadied her nerves. *I need a plan*, Lola thought. But she couldn't begin to think of what kind of plan a person should make under such circumstances.

"There," Peter said. "That's better, isn't it?"

He talked on about his scientific ideas, and Lola steered the conversation away from herself. What, after all, could she say now that was true? Not even her vital statistics were necessarily valid. Her birth date? It had not happened. Her history? There was none. She began to feel weightless and free, like a kite whose string has snapped.

"I think I get what you mean by bunkum," she said. "Like people who say aliens suck them up in their spaceships and do experiments on them."

"I haven't heard anything like that before," Peter said. "But I wouldn't discount it entirely. I'll bet there are moon men and Martians up there, millions of them maybe, going about their business, eating supper and driving their automobiles just like we are, and one day they might pay us a call. It only stands to reason."

Lola nodded politely and swallowed her mouthful of cider to keep it from shooting out of her nose, then pulled Peter back onto the dance floor. Despite the colossal weirdness of the situation, and the absolute violation of the laws of physics, she was enjoying herself very much—the music and the glitter and mainly this teen scientist in a man's suit. At last the orchestra played its final chord, and the dancers broke into applause.

"Don't go yet," Peter said. "Let's look at the stars."

A full moon lit up the campus, and the lawns glowed silver-green. Couples strolled along the paths. Snatches of their chatter floated along on the autumn-scented breeze.

"Here's a nice spot," Peter said. He brushed some leaves from the edge of the fountain and they sat down. Above them, a bronze mermaid—a mermaid with a head, a beautiful head with curly bronze tresses—spouted water through parted lips. The water bubbled and tinkled into a pool strewn with wishing pennies.

"Where do you live, Lola?"

"Quarrier Street." She was glad to be telling the truth at least this once. "I just moved in."

"You'll be attending school here at Ashfield, then?"

"Yes," she said.

"That is wonderful news. I hope you won't think us too dull. I mean, after New York. I'll bet our new dances are old hat to you."

Lola rubbed her ankles and made a face. "But they're all new hat to me. Couldn't you tell?"

"It's those French hobo shoes. They're no good for dancing the Lindy Hop. From a structural point of view, I mean. May I?"

He stretched Lola's right foot onto his wool-covered knee and pulled off her shoe and sock. The night air tickled her foot. "This is a peculiar stocking," he remarked, stretching the twenty-first-century microfiber up and down. "Stays up by itself, doesn't it? Is it rubber?"

"It's from France," Lola said. "Pretty soon—"

"I know, we'll all be wearing rubber socks."

He placed her bare foot under the cascade of cool water from the mermaid's mouth and rubbed the tendons with firm fingers. She closed her eyes and watched the fireworks exploding on the backs of her eyelids. Every thought, every fear, was knocked from her brain.

"May I make a personal observation?" Peter said.

"Go ahead."

"You seem foreign. I mean, not only from out of state but, I can't put my finger on it, like someone from another country. You're from far away. Am I right?"

"No. Domestic. Not an import," Lola said, but she loved that he'd asked. She looked foreign to him, exotic. Having been told it, she began to feel it.

"Maybe something about the way you talk. Something's different. I'm sure I'm right."

He put Lola's foot down and started in on the other one. All the while he watched her steadily. Finally, he shook his head and chuckled to himself.

"What?" Lola said.

"You're such a beautiful girl," he said. "I haven't bothered to look at the stars."

Members of the orchestra now moved across the lawn with their instrument cases, toward the dark street. "Closing up, kids," the singer called to them, then faded down the path until there was nothing left of him but his hum: *Every morning, every evening, ain't we got fun?*

"It's still early," Peter said. "We could go to my workshop and I'll fix your necklace. My house is down on the corner of Elm and Maple, just near here. Then I could walk you home, if you like.

Or we could meet up with some of the kids at the picnic grounds. We could get my telescope or—"

He held out his hand, and she took it, and a shock ran from her forehead to her toenails, as strong as a jolt of electricity but warm, thrilling. She knew he'd felt it, too, because he forgot what he was saying about the telescope and stared down at their clasped hands.

"Will you come, then?" he said shyly.

Lola nodded and stood up. "Let me grab my bag."

"Lola," he said as she moved away, carrying her shoes. "I almost didn't come to the dance tonight, but I'm so awful glad I did."

"So am I," Lola said.

"I'll wait for you," he called. "Right here, by the mermaid."

Lola raced into the gym. Groups of flushed and happy dancers jostled her as they filed out. Her bare feet slapped along the hallway. She rounded the corner, entered the library, and passed through the low doorway into the reserve room. She snatched her knapsack from the table and read the words *YOU SUCK.*

Three

The room had returned to its previous condition, with the moldy air and overflowing garbage bin. The long sofa was gone, along with the reading lamps and wide oak desk. She knew Peter would be gone, too, but she ran from the room to look for him, along corridors that had lost their sheen.

Voices, happy voices, echoed from the direction of the gym. The dancers? Could they still be there? She ran faster, her feet slapping painfully now on the cold floor.

She entered the gym. A stocky girl in a red vinyl mini-dress stood on a ladder, laughing at the disco ball that wouldn't come down, and the same student council doofs she'd seen earlier yanked at streamers and popped balloons. They all turned to look at her.

"It's over," the girl on the ladder shouted down to her. "Nobody's allowed back in."

Lola raced straight through the gym and out into the courtyard. In a second she was at the fountain, looking into its dry basin at a thousand dirty wads of gum. She dropped her shoes and sank to her knees in the dewy grass. Sweat trickled down her back. She was dizzy and held on to her hair with both hands to steady herself. The clock tower down the street tolled faintly. It was midnight. After a while she heard the one o'clock chime, and then the two o'clock, and then, after what seemed only a few minutes, three chimes came.

She noticed that she was shivering. If only she could go back inside, into the gym, for just a few minutes. She stood up. Her limbs were stiff and cramped. She got to the door and pulled on it.

It wouldn't open. She yanked harder and then kicked it. An alarm went off, loud and grinding.

She staggered back over to the fountain and sat down on the edge. A jingling made her look up. "Peter?" she called out.

A night watchman was approaching on the walk. "Who's over there?"

"Lola."

The beam of a flashlight struck her in the face and she turned away. She saw that the dew on the grass had turned to frost.

"Lola what?" the guard said.

"Lola Lundy."

"You alone?"

"Yeah."

"Who's Peter?"

"Nobody. I'm alone."

"Did you scream before? I thought I heard a scream."

Lola's ears rang as if she'd been at a rock concert. She wasn't sure if she'd screamed or not. She might have, she thought, when the alarm went off. She didn't answer.

"Whatcha doin' here?"

"I was helping clean the library. I think I fell asleep. I'm new."

"It's three-thirty in the morning. Did you know that?"

The alarm grated on and on. The guard raked his beam over her seated figure. The light lingered on her bare feet. "You been drinking alcohol this evening, Lola?"

"No." she lied, remembering the spiked cider.

He jingled the keys again. He had a potbelly that sagged over his belt. "You smoking anything, then?"

"No."

"Uh-huh. Where's your shoes?"

She looked around. The shoes were next to her in the grass. She held them up and tried to smile. "Here they are. I was just rinsing off my feet."

The guard pointed at the cracked, revolting basin. "In that?"

"I mean, I was going to wash my feet, until I saw it was empty. I'm new. I'm going home now."

The guard slowly nodded. He had accepted the story. He'd especially liked the ending, this weird girl's exit from his territory. He said a few words into his walkie-talkie and the alarm stopped ringing.

"You got a ride or something?"

She nodded toward the parking lot. "That's my bike over there."

"Yeah? Okay, then." He watched her get up.

She couldn't find her socks. She jammed on the shoes and started toward her bike.

The guard's voice came after her, through the dark. "By the way, you can't park there. That's staff only. Hey!"

Lola pedaled like crazy away from the school, not because of the night watchman but because she had suddenly remembered the yearbook. It was in her knapsack and she had to look at it, right away, now. At the first intersection she stopped under a streetlight and pulled out the book. Crumbs of paper flaked from the edges of its old pages and shot off into the wind as she leafed quickly through the senior class photos: *A-B-C-D-E-F-G-H-Haley-Hansen-Hemmings-Higgins-Hill. Peter Hemmings.* Peter looked at her from out of an oval frame, serious and grown-up in shades of gray. He had on the same suit he had worn at the dance; she knew the soft feel of its woolen sleeve. Her hand holding the page shook. "There you are," she whispered, but then she reread the heading on the page: *CLASS OF 1924.* It couldn't be "are." It had to be "were." But she had just seen him, just now, just danced with him, felt his hands, warm and alive and young, massaging her feet under the waterfall. Somewhere, she felt sure, *he still has to be,* somewhere nearby, but hidden.

She paged through the rest of the portraits. She found Luther "Thumbtack" Matthews, the image faded but recognizable, and then Whoopsie Whipple, looking solemn as a saint in her junior class portrait. Her real name was Mary.

A minivan passed through the intersection and startled her. She'd almost forgotten she was standing on a road. She thought of how she must look, a teenage girl loitering under a streetlight in the dead of night. The minivan dorks had probably reported her, and there she sat, breaking curfew in the most obvious available spot.

She zipped up the yearbook in her knapsack and veered down a side street. The detour passed through Fairview, a decaying neighborhood where it was dark and dense and easier to travel unnoticed. She and her mother had supposedly lived in a trailer park around here once, but she had no memory of it. She skimmed past ramshackle apartment buildings, vacant lots, and dark storefronts.

Soon she saw the abandoned brick factory ringed in barbed wire that marked her halfway point. A weak yellow streetlight shone down on the spooky ruin, and Lola read the familiar sign carved into the stone front: *GADD BRICKS.* The rhythm of her pedaling, the chilly wind, helped her calm down. How, she asked herself, had it happened? *How* does a person fall asleep in the twenty-first century, wake in 1923, attend a dance, turn over her favorite possession to a stranger with thrilling green eyes, and then, without any sort of warning, end up back in the present, barefoot, staring at the words *YOU SUCK* scratched into a tabletop? But these were questions for the head of NASA, not for somebody who had flunked gym.

She skidded up to the group home and locked her bike to the rack. Coming in so late was a serious crime, but that was a problem she'd face some other time. She swiped her keycard in the lock. It would record the time of her arrival: 3:51 A.M. Would Graham bother to look at the log? You never knew with her. Dottie Graham ran the Wrigley house with about as much animation as an iguana, but every once in a while she'd come to life and make a drug bust or enforce a rule. Lola crept up the stairs, encountering no one, and entered her room as quietly as she could. Danielle, her roommate, was asleep. Lola sat down on her bed, unzipped her knapsack, and brought out the yearbook. She couldn't wait until morning to look at it again. She found her miniature book light on the bedside table and switched it on.

Again she looked at the senior class, lingering longest on Peter's serious face. She closed her eyes and remembered the strange, warm shock that had passed between them. She paged forward and found a section dedicated to various school events: a home-coming game, a debate club tournament, a class picnic. Near the bottom of one of the pages she noticed the caption, "Fall Frolic, 1923." She moved the light closer. It was a big dance in the gym, with an orchestra. The musicians were the most prominent figures in the photo, and she began to examine them. The drummer with the long moustache was unmistakably the same one she'd seen at the dance. And the singer who'd gone humming into the dark, she recognized him, too. What if . . . ?

The dance floor was a blurred mass of heads and legs; she could identify no one. Then she saw it: a dark object on a chair. Could it be her cap? Yes, she thought, it had to be.

A thin, drowsy voice came from the other bed: "Lola?"

Lola jumped and found herself juggling the book light. The beam swept crazily around the room. "Danielle. You're awake."

"You yelled," Danielle said.

"No. You were dreaming." The upturned beam of the book light shone full on Lola's lap.

"What's that?"

"An old book I found in the trash."

"Lemme see it."

Lola slid the yearbook back into her bag. She didn't like the idea of anybody else touching it.

"You can't read it in bed like that."

"Why not?"

"It's delicate. It'll fall apart." Lola zipped up the knapsack and hung it on its usual hook between the beds.

"You weren't in the dining hall," Danielle said. She was more awake now.

"Yeah. I fell asleep in the library. Nobody woke me up, so I was there a long time."

Danielle glanced at the clock. "Oh my God, it's almost four in the morning." She seemed to be scrutinizing Lola now. "Where have you really been? With a guy? It's a guy, isn't it? Tell me."

"I did tell you," Lola said. She wanted the conversation to end so she could think. She changed into an oversized T-shirt, got in bed, and turned off the book light.

"You're hiding something from me," Danielle said. Lola heard her roll over. Seconds later she was snoring softly.

But Lola was spinning, confused, sparkling, afraid. She felt she would not sleep that night, might never sleep again. Theories were forming, dissolving, reforming faster than she could process them. Her cap was in that picture. That meant she must be in that swirling crowd, she and Peter. It was impossible, ridiculous, but it had happened. She closed her eyes and seemed to hear the music again, bouncy, carefree.

Every morning, every evening, ain't we got fun?

For a long time she listened to it and seemed to feel his hands again, holding her feet under the water. The fireworks came again, this time somewhere deep in her chest. Just before dawn she fell asleep.

Four

The next day was Saturday, the day of Lola's morning shift at Golden Recipe Fried Chicken. She stayed in bed. Work seemed irrelevant now. Everything seemed irrelevant, repulsive, even. She'd defied the laws of the universe and now she was supposed to go fry chicken in a strip mall?

Danielle was so curious about Lola's funk that she trembled like a Chihuahua around her bed, yapping out questions. "Where were you last night? Where were you *really*? Is that why you're in such a bad mood? You have to go to work. Terry'll fire you for sure. He was thinking about it, you know, after you chucked that biscuit at the wall. Don't you give a shit? You're not pregnant, are you?" At last Danielle gave up and went down to breakfast, then left to meet her cousin Beth, who lived in town.

As soon as Danielle's bus vanished around the corner, Lola brought the knapsack down from its hook and took out the yearbook. She wanted to immerse herself in it the way she'd done in the night, wallow in it, drown in it, but she couldn't even open the cover. The mere feel of the thing in her hands brought on a scorching grief. She put it away.

All morning she lay in bed, staring at the grid pattern on the ceiling with its brown water stain in one corner that looked like a rat. The secret seemed to be growing like a parasite inside her, getting heavier and bigger. She could almost feel it pushing at her skin, pricking and prodding and itching. The feeling had been so strong that morning that she'd nearly dropped a hint to Danielle. But she'd held back. Danielle was the wrong person to tell. She couldn't keep her mouth shut. What Lola needed was someone discreet and open-minded. A nuclear physicist. That was it. Maybe she could phone a radio call-in program and speak anonymously with an expert. They could go over the facts point by point. She sat up sharply and swung her legs over the side of the bed. Maybe she could find a program on Public Radio, and then . . . who was she kidding? They would only think she was nuts, or that it was a prank call. She dropped back down on the bed and curled up in a ball. For several hours she lay still, and refused to come down for lunch.

Danielle and Beth showed up in the afternoon, and Danielle chattered, silly and flushed, about Brent Gaynor, her longtime unrequited love, for what seemed like twenty-four hours. Beth, a big girl with hairy forearms and lots of pimples, hung on every word as Danielle described Brent Gaynor's walk, his "cute" gestures, his new jeans, his "sublime" butt, his latest haircut, then his butt again. Danielle sketched a diagram in two colors of ink showing the happy points where their class schedules intersected, and the sad points where they did not. For at least twenty minutes, the girls tried to decrypt the meaning behind Brent Gaynor's "How's it going, Danielle?" greeting of last Friday, which had replaced his customary "Hey."

Several times Lola thought she might literally have to vomit. At last the cousins went to Taco Bell and left her in peace.

Graham barged in that evening to see what was going on. Lola said she'd caught a virus, and tried to sound congested. Graham accepted the story and promptly excused herself; *Makeup Disasters* was about to come on. Secretly, Lola had decided never to get out of bed again. She could not imagine any point to anything. Had she glimpsed that other life, tasted it, tried it on, only to be shut out of it forever? At night she could not sleep and spent the long hours while Danielle snored teasing apart every nuance of that Friday night in 1923.

The days went by. She found it agreeably numbing to hold still, like the Earth's axis, and let everyone else spin around her. Morning buses picked people up at the bus stop below her window, and afternoon buses dropped the same people off again. Danielle got dressed and undressed and dressed again. The sun made its daily transit around the ceiling.

And then, on Wednesday, Hershey showed up.

"I know you aren't asleep," the social worker said, standing at the foot of Lola's bed. "It's not a bad performance, but I've seen better."

Lola heard the springs of Danielle's bed creak and realized Hershey was parking herself for a while. This didn't bode well.

"Want to talk about it?" Hershey said.

Lola rolled over to face the wall. "About what?"

"The reason you haven't been in school for three days. You look like a zombie, by the way."

Lola knew from ample experience that no good lie could be told without eye contact. She rolled back over and opened her eyes. Hershey was sitting there chewing an extra-strength Rolaids. As usual her glasses were smudged and her sweater was buttoned wrong; Hershey was kind of a mess.

Sound sane, Lola told herself. *Sound normal.*

"I thought I was getting an ulcer," Lola stated. "I kept getting these stomach aches every time I ate something, see. That's why I decided to stay in bed." She tried for that congested voice again, but it didn't sound as good as when she'd used it on Graham. Any voice would be okay, she thought, as long as it wasn't a crazy-sounding one. She would not risk sounding crazy. Not ever. It was what everybody expected of her, what they were all watching for, and she wouldn't give it to them.

"An ulcer," Hershey said. "Uh-huh." She got up and wandered around the room, looking at Lola's hairbrush and her Kleenex box and the other personal items on her bureau. Finally, she sat down at the foot of Lola's bed. "Maybe you'd like to talk to someone."

Lola sat up. "I'm not crazy, goddammnit!" she screamed. She had vowed not to scream and now she had. She hated herself.

"Calm down. No one said you were crazy."

"I won't go to Hillside. I won't set foot in there."

"Not even to talk? An informal chat? Just to get things off your chest? Hillside does have some very qualified people."

Lola wrestled her way out of the tangled sheets. "I was about to do my laundry. The migraine's mostly gone and—"

"Migraine?"

"Ulcer. The ulcer brought on a migraine. I've got school tomorrow, so if you don't mind—"

"You wanna know what I think?" Hershey interrupted, recrossing her legs.

Lola braced herself for some "tough love" or perhaps an inspirational slogan: *Turn your wounds into wisdom. Life is what you make it. Never quit.*

"I don't think you've got an ulcer, or a migraine. I think maybe your pain's somewhere else. Like in here." Hershey indicated the ruffle on the front of her polka-dot polyester blouse. "It's been hard to adjust to the group-home setting. It doesn't feel like a home. Maybe nowhere feels like home. But think of it this way— someday you'll make a home. It's something you can look forward to.

"People like me don't have homes," Lola said. She'd managed to keep her voice down this time, but inside she was screaming: *I think I know where my home should be! I saw it, but I can't get there! I can't get home!* Because the long days and nights since the dance had led Lola to a devastating conviction: She did not belong in this time. Her place was in another century, and the powers of the universe had conspired to reveal this mistake to her. In that other place, she'd fit in. She'd felt new and clean, her true self.

Hershey talked on and on, perched at the foot of the bed, but Lola didn't hear anything. She didn't need to hear anything. She was trapped in a "now" that had nothing to do with her, where she would always be something grotesque, a joke of a person. Her thinking always circled around to the same question: What could she do with this knowledge, other than be tortured by it?

It seemed like about four hours before Hershey finally stood up, and another two before she shut up and disappeared out the door. But Lola knew she'd be back, and soon. Like it or not, her time in bed was over.

She scraped some random clothes off the floor, got dressed, and dragged herself down to the dining hall. She tried to look ordinary as she picked at her square of lasagna, but the grief was worse than ever. It sat like an anvil across her shoulders, pressing her toward the floor. She was a ratty-haired phantasm in a stained sweatshirt, and everybody stared at her, even Jared Fantino, the guy who'd sneaked a stick of dynamite into the bowling alley and generally had no interest in anything whatsoever.

She moved through the next day in a fog. At school, she accepted the make-up assignments with a nod, all the time certain that she was too far behind even to attempt them. Hershey's voice was a low buzz in her ear: *What will you do when you turn eighteen? It's less than two years from now. You'll be an adult then. What will you do? What will you do? What will you do?*

Lunch seemed nauseating and pointless—why eat?—so she went to the gym and sat on the bleachers. She closed her eyes. With a little concentration she could bring forth the silly, happy music that had played in that very room.

Every morning, every evening
Ain't we got fun?
Not much money, oh, but honey
Ain't we got fun?

She descended the bleachers and stepped to the center of the gym. Her feet began to move. *One-two-three-and-four.* The Lindy Hop. She remembered it perfectly. Her arms reached out for her invisible partner. *Five. Rotate. Seven-and-eight.* The orchestra came closer, clearer, until it seemed to be assembled just on the other side of a flimsy partition. Soon she could pick out the individual instruments: a clarinet, a trumpet, a pair of saxophones that wove in and out like ribbon candy. And then from somewhere entered giggling that didn't belong.

Lola stopped dancing.

A group of freshman girls in basketball uniforms had come in from the locker rooms. How long had they been watching her? The music warped and faded as Lola fled the gym. Her throat constricted. The tears came and wouldn't stop. She ran all the way to the parking lot, to her bike. She would miss algebra and a history test, but she couldn't worry about that now. She'd worry another time.

Safely back in her room with the door shut, she pulled out the yearbook. It still hurt to look at it, but the hurt was good now, like seeing a picture of home when you're far away. The mermaid appeared on page 1. The fall dance was pictured on pages 28 and 29. Peter Hemmings appeared on pages 6, 11, 17, 24, and 26. His page numbers were like the combination to a treasure vault.

After a while Danielle showed up and sat around reading the new *Vogue*. This time Lola didn't bother to hide the yearbook. Why should she?

"Reading that book from the garbage again?" Danielle said.

"I guess," Lola said.

"What's so interesting about it?"

"The clothes."

Danielle slid off her bed and came over to take a look. "You're right. Some of that's back in style." She waved the *Vogue* at Lola. "Beads are in now. And that plunging neckline, I'd wear that."

Lola turned to page 23 to show Danielle the picture of the stylish girls' glee club. Danielle traced her finger down a bear-like fur coat on one of the girls in the front row. She was a curly-haired girl, waving a pennant and laughing.

"They look just like us," Danielle said. "It's a shame."

"What is?"

"That all these kids are dead now."

Lola felt like she'd been punched in the kidneys. She wanted to argue, but of course it was perfectly true to Danielle, to everybody else.

"I wonder what happened to them all," Danielle said. "After they got out of school, I mean."

They're still in school. Don't worry. I just saw them, Lola thought.

"Probably a bunch of them died in one of those world wars," Danielle went on.

The words brought a sweat to Lola's forehead. She felt woozy and was glad she was sitting down. *No, they didn't die. They didn't.*

"And diseases," Danielle said. "There weren't any shots, you know. They all got polio and romantic fever. And that black plague. Probably that killed off a lot of them. About a hundred billion people died of that. I saw it on TV. Their tongues turned black and swelled up and then—"

Lola slapped the yearbook shut and stuffed it back in her knapsack.

"What?" Danielle said.

"I'm bored."

Danielle sneezed. "Moldy."

On Saturday morning Lola put on her ill-fitting uniform of yellow polyester—the pants too big and the top too small—shouldered her knapsack, and pedaled over to Golden Recipe Fried Chicken.

As usual, she took the back roads to avoid the municipal sports complex and its parking lot full of SUVs. She couldn't stand seeing the school cliques hanging around in their soccer or tennis clothes, taking pictures of each other, laughing, eating the kind of fun, crappy fast food it was her job to prepare. As much as she hated seeing them, it was worse if they saw her ride by in her ugly uniform. Her stomach squeezed into something black and hard then, and it took an hour for it to stop hurting.

Mr. Terry, the manager, saw her coming through the egg-shaped entrance and quickly checked his watch. His face fell when he saw she was on time.

Mr. Terry had been a schoolteacher, but for some reason nobody knew, he wasn't one anymore. Lola assumed he was your garden-variety pervert, but whatever the case, he talked of his teaching days as a lost paradise where he'd been respected and had wielded authority, and of the present as an undeserved purgatory among frozen chickens and smartass subordinates.

Today he was in a tizzy; the janitorial service had crashed its van and couldn't sterilize the restrooms until further notice. Terry could have picked any of the five employees to fill in, but he fixed on Lola. It was revenge, she figured, for her unexplained absence the week before.

"Let's shake a leg, people," he said, striding uselessly about the kitchen. Mr. Terry never did any work himself; he just hovered and bossed. He had a way of standing ramrod straight and flexing his butt muscles inside his yellow polyester pants while he yelled at people. No wonder they wouldn't let him teach school.

Lola gathered her courage and flung open the restroom doors. Since their last cleaning, the stalls had been the scene of any number of biological and recreational events, and the grossness had reached a new high. The trashcans overflowed onto the slimy floor, and one of the toilets was stuffed to the brim with Golden Recipe wet-wipes—somebody's idea of a joke. Flies buzzed in the stalls. Lola held her breath and worked as fast as she could, blindly sloshing hot water and disinfectant toward spots that were too awful to be viewed by human eyes.

The rest of the shift was a blur of greasy chicken parts set to Muzak. At four o'clock she tore off her hairnet and went to get her paycheck. She found Mr. Terry in the stifling storage room he referred to as his "office." It reeked of ammonia, chicken fat, and Mr. Terry's stale breath. She hovered in the doorway.

"Come on in," he said, poking away at his adding machine. "What can I do you for?"

Lola took a step toward Mr. Terry and noticed, as she had on other occasions, how he seemed to be steadily turning yellow—his hair, his skin, the whites of his eyes—to match the wallpaper, the buttermilk biscuits, the ancient oil in the deep fryer. "I'd like my paycheck, please," she said.

Mr. Terry didn't look up. "Paycheck?" he repeated as if trying out a new word.

"It should be fifty-eight dollars, more or less, by my calculations," Lola said.

"Your calculations, you say." The yellow man chuckled, gesturing for Lola to sit down on the lone metal folding chair that faced his desk.

Lola ventured into the room with creeping dread. The manager's tone, the office setting, reminded her of the times she'd been kicked out of school. She sat down and squinted at him across the desk. He got up and shut the door. She tensed. Maybe he was about to try for a grope session, in which case she was fully prepared to knock his yellow teeth straight up through the roof of his mouth.

Mr. Terry sat down on the corner of his desk, way too close to her chair. His thighs seemed to hover right in her face. The polyester gripped the contours of his crotch in a way that would be good for a nightmare or two later on. He plucked a pencil from his desk and tasted the eraser. Lola caught a glimpse of the slimy underside of his tongue and shivered.

"Let me tell you a little bit about *my* calculations, Lola," he said.

Now she understood: Despite the crotch in her face, this wasn't entirely a perv thing. He was drawing out the delivery of some yummy nugget of bad news and savoring her discomfort.

"You broke a light fixture last month. Remember *that?*"

"It fell and almost hit me," she shot back.

Terry raised his eyebrows in fake surprise. He sauntered around his desk and sat down. His chair groaned as he leaned back and folded his arms behind his head. "Hmm. How I remember it is that you threw a biscuit at it and broke it."

She had thrown a biscuit. That much was true. But it was only to let off some steam and to demonstrate the cement-like texture of Golden Recipe baked goods to a new coworker. She had missed the light fixture by a foot at least. The next day, when the same light fixture fell, Mr. Terry blamed the "delayed seismic reverberations" from Lola's biscuit attack. She never dreamed he'd take it this far.

"It cost us seventy-nine ninety-nine to replace that fixture. So the good news is you'll be done working it off by the end of next week."

Lola felt every muscle in her body contract. She wanted to scream, to commit murder. She would have leaped across the desk and administered a tracheotomy with a flexible drink straw if it hadn't been such an obvious felony.

But then she saw him watching her, his mouth open, his teeth bared, his eyebrows raised, in anticipation of her protest, her tears. She smiled blandly. "That seems more than fair, Mr. Terry," she said. "Yes, indeed, it certainly does."

His chair brought him bolt upright with a shriek. He was startled speechless. Lola had popped him like a balloon. His day was ruined.

"Okay, then," he blustered. "I hope you've learned your lesson."

"Oh, I have . . . *sir.*" She wanted to add, "By the way, I quit," but felt this would only tickle the old butt-flexer. So she quit without saying it. He'd figure it out when he was short-handed during the next lunch rush.

On the way out, she paused in the employee break room just long enough to jimmy open the manager's locker and remove two crisp fifty-dollar bills from Terry's wallet. Sixty dollars was for her work and the other forty for the emotional distress she'd suffered in the putrid closet. He was getting off easy. She slipped the empty wallet back into his pocket. Gag—the operation had called for contact with the seat of Terry's tan chinos. She replaced the lock carefully so that it appeared untouched. Skills acquired in juvenile hall so often came in handy.

On the way home she stopped at the Dollar Store and bought a magnifying glass. Her plan was to rush upstairs, shut herself in her room, and spend the afternoon alone with the yearbook. She had looked at it all Friday afternoon and into the evening, and had held it tight against her as she slept. She had carried it to work in her knapsack and taken a peek at it on her break, out back by the trashcans, after cleaning the bathrooms. With a magnifying glass she could see the object that might be her cap more clearly, and maybe she could make out a few more faces.

She couldn't seem to leave the yearbook alone. It was the thread that connected her to that place where she was foreign, interesting, more beautiful than the stars, the place where a young scientist had waited beside a bronze mermaid. How long, she wondered, had he waited there for her?

Five

In the parking lot of the Dollar Store, Lola decided not to go straight home. Graham might be lying in wait for her with the new chore rotation. And Danielle was meeting Beth again for a Brent Gaynor worship service. There was Hershey to consider as well. She had an annoying habit of popping by and scrutinizing her like she was trying to read her mind. It always left Lola feeling guilty, whether she'd done anything or not. She had to go somewhere else, a place she'd be left in peace.

She rode around randomly for a while, coasting through the better neighborhood with the new condos and then heading through Fairview, which just got worse and worse. So many of the houses were vacant, or had their front porches falling off or a beat-up dishwasher dumped in the front yard or rancid beach towels hung up where curtains should have been. Ashfield had prospered once as one of Ohio's main steel and quarry towns. But that was ages ago, and now entire boulevards were taken up by abandoned factories, weedy lots, and windowless saloons that hid behind dirty brick facades.

Sometimes when she rode through Fairview Lola found herself wondering why she couldn't remember living there. It had been three or four years of her life, but it was a blank slate. Even the memories of her mother were so faint now that she couldn't be certain they weren't her own inventions; she wasn't sure whether to be angry she couldn't remember or glad. She spun past the public library. As usual, all sorts of dumbasses were hanging out in the parking lot; a fat guy in a velour sweatsuit yelled something at her she couldn't make out while the others laughed. After a while Lola stopped to rest in the one halfway decent place she could think of, Ashfield City Park. It had cannons, a few flower beds, and a couple of granite monuments. She found a nice place to sit on top of one of the cannons, right next to a sign that read, *DO NOT SIT ON CANNONS*. She had just begun to unzip her knapsack when she felt raindrops. Her first thought was to protect the yearbook. She knew the devastating effect of water on old paper. Her tattered knapsack wasn't equal to the job.

Lightning flashed and the sprinkle became a downpour. She had to find shelter. Across the street were a few junk stores she'd never noticed before. She grabbed her bike and made for the closest one. The sign on the door read, *YESTERDAY BOUTIQUE*.

Lola entered a wide carpeted space like a lobby and guessed that the building had once been a movie theater. As her eyes adjusted to the dim light, her guess was confirmed by a rinky-dink museum dedicated to the building's past. The first exhibit was a snack bar with an antique popcorn popper, vintage candy boxes, and a big brass cash register. A few steps beyond, an ancient movie projector and a row of plush red seats were displayed behind a velvet security rope. Lola crouched to read a sign hanging from the rope: *These original furnishings were salvaged from The Grand Theater, which opened on this spot on Memorial Day, 1915, and closed Dec. 21, 1974. Modeled in a combination of French Baroque and Rococo styles, the theater was designed to resemble opera houses and palaces of Europe of the sixteenth and seventeenth centuries. It was an important social hub in Ashfield for many years. Although most of the contents of the theater, including its Mighty Wurlitzer organ (built 1919), were sold at auction in early 1975, the Ashfield Historical Society obtained these few pieces for the benefit of posterity. Please do not touch.*

Lola stood back up. Several black-and-white photos of the theater in its heyday hung on the wall behind the seats. She leaned over the rope for a closer look. One picture showed a line of patrons snaking away from the ticket booth. *THE SHEIK*, the marquee read, starring a certain Rudolph Valentino. He was dressed in Arabian robes and had a woman in his arms, tipped backward in a suffocating kiss. Lola was studying the kiss when a terrific thunderclap sounded overhead. The lights flickered.

"Ah, Valentino."

Lola jerked around.

A small old lady in a psychedelic floral pantsuit and a crooked, honey-colored wig stood close behind her, peering over her shoulder. The lady pulled a pair of big square glasses from her pocket for a closer examination.

"And of course when he died in 1926, one hundred thousand people attended his funeral," the woman said, giving Lola the odd impression that they had been standing there chatting about Valentino all day long. "Pola Negri was so overcome with grief that she fainted right into his open casket—several times, in fact."

"Paula?"

"Not Paula, dear, Pola. Pola Negri, the silent film star. Some people claimed it was a publicity stunt, but don't you believe it." The woman looked sad about this Valentino business and Lola worried she might be about to cry. She thought she better change the subject.

"So this was a theater, huh?" she asked, and tried to look interested in the answer.

"It was called The Grand, and a great showplace it was, too," sighed the lady, whose name tag read, "Miss Bryant." "It closed in 1974, right after they built the Springfield fourplex." She lowered her voice to a whisper. "By the end, they were playing only the dirty movies, if you know what I mean."

"Pornos," Lola whispered back, and the woman nodded regretfully.

Lola looked beyond Miss Bryant, through an open set of doors quilted in red leather, to where the theater seating had once stood. Rows of clothing racks sloped toward a stage cluttered with junk. The impression was that of an enormous garage sale tilted on its side.

"Looking for anything in particular?" Miss Bryant asked, her magnified eyes bobbing under the big lenses.

Lola thought it might be rude to say that she'd only come in to get out of the rain, so she said she'd stopped by to browse and descended the cluttered slope of racks arranged by decade. She came first to a forest of taffeta cocktail dresses from the 1940s—a few still bearing the stains of some long-forgotten champagne toast—and then roamed into a neighborhood of 1950s petticoats. She turned and meandered into a far corner near the stage. Then she saw something that stopped her cold: It was Whoopsie Whipple's pink silk dress, or one just like it. The dress jutted out from the end of a rack as if, like Whoopsie herself, it wanted to be discovered. Lola reached out and rolled the fringed hem between her fingers. It felt fragile as a moth and reminded her of the yearbook. She checked inside the collar on the chance that somebody had sewn a name label into it. There was none. It sure looked like Whoopsie's, though. She sniffed the fabric. It smelled of old perfume and mothballs.

"Eighteen ninety-nine," said a voice. Miss Bryant had sneaked up on her again.

Lola jerked her nose out of the dress.

"That's the price, of course, not the vintage," the old lady added.

"1923, maybe?" Lola ventured.

Miss Bryant gripped her wig in excitement. Lola's guess was exactly right. Might she be a fellow history buff? "How I do adore the Roaring Twenties. It's one of my favorite historical decades. The Jazz Age. Flappers. Flagpole-sitting. Al Capone and the bootleggers."

"Was that a band?"

Miss Bryant looked bewildered. "You don't mean you've never heard of Prohibition?"

"You mean probation," Lola said. "That's a punishment you get instead of jail."

"Oh dear. Oh my. No. Prohibition made alcoholic drinks illegal from 1920 to 1933 by Constitutional amendment, the 18th Amendment. Memorize that. Have you?"

"1920 to 1933. The 18th Amendment," Lola repeated. "Beer was illegal? That's hard to believe."

"I know whereof I speak," Miss Bryant said. "I'm the president of the Ashfield Historical Society. Don't they teach history anymore?"

"Maybe it doesn't stick," Lola answered, scraping aside the hanger that held the pink dress. Time had reduced the next few garments to faded scraps of silk and organdy. "What was that you said about sitting on flagpoles?"

Miss Bryant nodded knowingly, disappeared into the confusion for a minute or two, and returned with a large framed photograph of a man in a suit and tie sitting on a platform mounted atop a flagpole. She looked pleased with herself.

"Flagpole-sitting was one of the great fads of the 1920s. The record was set in 1930 by Mr. Bill Penfield," Miss Bryant said, pausing to indicate the man in the photo. "He sat on this flagpole in Strawberry Point, Iowa, for fifty-one days and twenty hours until a thunderstorm brought him down."

"Who knows how long he might have stayed up there otherwise?" Lola commented. It was the only thing she could think of to say.

"Indeed, who knows?" Miss Bryant agreed, leaning the photo against a pillar. "Of course, by then the fad had gone right out of style."

"Of course," Lola nodded. She turned away from Mr. Penfield on the pole and pushed aside the next hanger. A sleeveless shift of pale green silk was revealed, the beads along its "V" neckline still managing to twinkle a little in their old age. It was slinky and feminine, not her kind of thing, but she reached out for it, and draped it along the front of her.

"Ravishing," Miss Bryant said. "You look just exactly like a flapper. Hmm. Except for the hair. Back then the bob was in style."

"No long hair?"

"Certainly not. The bob meant freedom, modernity, fun. Long hair was old-fashioned, stuffy, restrictive, like long dresses and corsets, something from the past."

Lola ran a hand down her ponytail. She didn't like it so much anymore.

Next to the flapper rack sat a wicker basket of long gloves in various conditions and colors. Lola tried on a pair of white ones, then picked up the silk dress again and admired the way the gloves went with it. Glancing down, Lola caught sight of the scuffed basketball shoes she'd saved up so long for last year. They looked big and stupid in the company of the dress. She turned toward Miss Bryant, who had climbed up on a stepladder and was rearranging the specimens on a hat rack.

"Excuse me," Lola said. "What's a hobo, exactly? Is it any different from a bum?"

Miss Bryant took a man's top hat from the rack and put it on, as if this would help her think better. "The hobo wasn't a bum," she began. "He had a creed and a work ethic. He rode the high iron far and wide and composed campfire ditties of enduring social relevance."

Lola nudged at a floorboard with her toe. "Do I . . . look like a hobo?"

Miss Bryant examined Lola from under the hat brim. "You look nothing whatsoever like a hobo. For starters, you'd need a banjo, or at the very least a harmonica, and a red kerchief with all your worldly goods bundled inside, hanging on a stick."

"A stick?"

"Or a hoe."

"Oh," Lola said, and turned back to her browsing.

But the hobo question had got Miss Bryant's attention. She adjusted her glasses to look more closely at Lola. It was rare for a young customer to ask such an exceptional question. "Just passing through?" she asked.

"No. I live here," Lola answered. "In the Wrigley home." The instant she said "Wrigley" she regretted it. The word meant "unhinged delinquent" in Ashfield and frightened people off. But with Miss Bryant it seemed to have the opposite effect.

"Ah, Old Judge Wrigley's place. I know it well. Used to visit the rose garden when I was little."

"Not *that* Wrigley place. I mean the group home. On Quarrier Street."

Miss Bryant took Lola by the arm. "Let me show you something."

She ushered Lola to a roped-off staircase with a sign across it that read, *NO ENTRY.* Miss Bryant moved the rope aside and led Lola up a curving set of stairs.

In a moment they were in the balcony. Lola was shocked. The place was piled floor to ceiling in Yesterday Boutique junk: overstuffed trunks and boxes, books and bundles, packages, chests and papers and crates. Miss Bryant disappeared right into the pile, like a deer into a thicket, and Lola saw that a path had been blazed through it, narrow and twisting, but definitely leading somewhere.

Lola followed, the path leading up and up under her feet, until they arrived at a narrow door reading, *PROJECTION BOOTH.* Miss Bryant took out a set of keys and unlocked it. They stepped inside. The rectangular room was filled with even more stuff—old film cans, oddball appliances, stacks of magazines. There was a mink cape with genuine teeth, baskets of doorknobs, a bag of bags, two bed warmers, a yoke for oxen, and six or seven broken cuckoo clocks hung all in a row. But there was also a tiny, tidy bedroom at the far end furnished with a single bed, an antique floor lamp, and a little round rag-rug. It reminded Lola of a bedroom in a dollhouse.

"You *live* here?" Lola blurted out, then worried it might have been rude to ask.

"Shh," she said. "I'm not supposed to, zoning laws and all. If the city found out, I'd be in trouble."

Miss Bryant turned and yanked open an old refrigerator. To Lola's surprise, it was crammed with books.

"I did have a house once, a nice warm little house," Miss Bryant said. "But it was hard to come up with the payment month after month, and business here, well, it's not as good as you might think. Anyway, it's a dull story. I'm making do all right."

She opened one of the fruit drawers, rooted around, and brought out an old volume. "Yes, yes. Here we are," she said, and sat down on a celery crate, daintily, like it was some kind of gorgeous silk tuffet.

Lola sat down on the cinder block next to it and watched Miss Bryant leaf through the pages of the book she'd selected. Lola was beginning to see that the Yesterday Boutique was not the nutty jumble that it seemed but a highly organized affair that made complete sense to Miss Bryant—crazy, but with a pattern, like her psychedelic pantsuit.

"Aha. Looky here," Miss Bryant said.

Lola leaned in. It was a picture of the Wrigley house. Her house. A white-haired couple stood by the front door. "Judge Horace and Eunice Vance Wrigley, 1948," the caption read.

Lola skimmed the text. These Wrigley people built the house in 1921 and left it to the county in their will. How funny to think the name Wrigley wasn't always associated with juvenile delinquency.

Lola pulled the new magnifying glass out of her jacket pocket and took a closer look. The fancy carved front door was unknown to her. It had been changed somewhere along the line for the metal-and-safety-glass model, the one with the tattletale keycard-swipe entry. She turned to the next page, which showed several pictures of the interior. She couldn't believe it. Her house hadn't always been a chopped-up maze of linoleum cubicles. It hadn't always had those low, plastic ceilings with the fluorescent sticks inside, that sickening green paint. It was once an airy, graceful mansion.

"And here's the rose garden," Miss Bryant said, turning the page. "The Wrigley roses. An acre of roses. They covered the whole back lawn. People came from far and wide to see them in the summer. The Wrigleys didn't have any children. They put all their love into the roses, I guess."

Lola thought about the noisy car dealership that now covered the ground where the roses had once grown. It butted right up against the group home and reeked of tires. The stink made you never want to open the back windows. She was about to mention the dealership but stopped herself; Miss Bryant probably preferred to remember the rose garden as it had been all those summers when she was little.

The next pages showed pictures of a neat little brick downtown. It took Lola a few seconds to realize that she was looking at Ashfield. She skimmed through the rest of the book, surprised by the wide-open fields that ran all the way to the edges of town and the dusty two-lane roads that crisscrossed the center. Lola closed the book and handed it back to Miss Bryant, who returned it to the fruit drawer and slammed the refrigerator.

In a moment they were back at the replica snack bar.

"Thanks," Lola said. "Your store is interesting. Way better than the mall."

"Why, thank you," Miss Bryant said. "Come back anytime. Tell your friends."

Lola nodded and stepped outside. It was dusk. The rain had stopped, but it was cold and windy. She worked the combination on her bike lock and it clicked open. She was about to remove the chain when an idea came to her, so clear and alive that it was more like a voice than an idea: *Buy the green dress, Lola.* She dropped the chain and let it dangle as the voice got louder, more assured: *You want the dress. You have the money. You should have the dress, the gloves. Buy them. Buy them, Lola.*

She rushed back through the double doors, not even bothering to lock up her bike. She made straight for the 1920s rack, Miss Bryant jogging after her. Lola chose the dress she'd admired, plus one blouse, one skirt, one bell-shaped hat, a string of fake pearls, and the only pair of shoes in the store that would fit her twenty-first-century feet. The shoes were a bargain at eighty-nine cents plus tax. In a dark corner of the stage under a pile of tennis rackets, she found several antique-looking suitcases and chose one of them. In a glass case near the cash register, she impulsively picked out a beaded coin purse with five old silver dollars inside.

She paid for the goods with Terry's two fifty-dollar bills. It was good to be rid of the money, of anything that had been that close to Terry's butt. She stuffed her loot into the suitcase and said goodbye to Miss Bryant a second time. Then she mounted her bike and wheeled off, shifting and reshifting her whimsical cargo into balance.

When she glanced back, Miss Bryant's hand was changing the sign from "Yes, We're Open" to "Sorry, We're Closed."

Six

Danielle was out, so Lola changed into the green dress, the hat, and the gloves. She leaned back on the bed and stared at one of her arms with a feeling that was new to her. What was this feeling? Happiness? Excitement? *No*, she thought. *It's delight.* She was delighted. It wasn't just how the glove looked; it was how it made her feel, like someone marvelous out of a movie, like that Pola Negri woman. She twirled the fake pearls. "Valentino, you were the great love of my life. I fainted at your funeral, you know, twice in fact, maybe even three times, and I wasn't even faking it," she was saying aloud just as Danielle opened the door.

Danielle looked at Lola, the blue eyes wide in her bony face. "What's going on?" She dropped her purse on the bed and moved to investigate. Danielle was always moving to investigate.

Lola yanked off the gloves. "Nothing."

Danielle scrutinized the old clothes. Lola could almost hear her brain cogs grinding away.

"Does this have something to do with that old yearbook?" Danielle asked, and began to giggle. "Are you trying to be like one of those people in that yearbook? You *are*."

"Yearbook?" Lola said, turning away from Danielle. She felt a hot blush come over her face. "No."

"Well, what's with the dress, then?"

"Halloween," Lola said casually.

"You're going as what?" Danielle re-examined the outfit. "An olden-days person?"

"A flapper. From the 1920s. Haven't you ever heard of the flappers?"

"Then this *is* about the yearbook."

"Maybe I got the idea there," Lola said.

Danielle came closer and breathed on her dress. "It's not a bad idea. In fact, it's a halfway decent idea. Wish I'd thought of it myself." She stroked Lola's hat with her pinky, like it was a new pet. "But I'm surprised you'd want to go to any school dance. You always say that stuff's for imbeciles."

"People do change," Lola said in a tone she thought Pola Negri might employ.

Then Danielle noticed the suitcase open on the bed and inside it the coin purse and the other old garments. "Where'd you find all this junk?"

The word stung. It wasn't junk.

"Downtown," Lola said. "In a big thrift store. The Yesterday Boutique, it's called."

"Did they have any other outfits like this? I want one, too."

"No," Lola lied.

Danielle pulled off her T-shirt and put on the vintage blouse. Lola bit her lip as Danielle struck poses in front of the mirror.

"Don't rip it," Lola said.

"And you need all this for one Halloween party?" Danielle demanded, turning to inspect the suitcase and its contents. She opened up the coin purse, took out the silver dollars, and jingled them in her cupped hands. "Wow. How much was all this?"

"Enough." Lola wrenched the coins from Danielle's hand and dropped them back into the purse. If only she'd heard Danielle coming she could have hidden everything. But Danielle was so light, so thin. She came and went as softly as a spider.

"Come on. What's the suitcase for, Lola?"

"I told you." In truth, Lola didn't know why she had bought so many things, but felt there was some vital reason, just beyond her understanding. She longed for a diversion: a bolt of lightning, a phone call. If Jared Fantino had appeared in the doorway right then to show off his stack of survivalist magazines, she might have been glad.

Danielle took off the blouse and dropped it on Lola's bed.

"Okay. Then who's your date?" Danielle asked, pulling her own shirt back on.

Lola turned away and pretended to tidy her desk. "I don't know yet. Anyway, you don't have to have a date."

"So you're wearing two olden-days outfits on the same night, or is this for two Halloweens, or two different Halloween parties?"

Suddenly Danielle was the district attorney conducting a cross-examination. It was time for a clever change of subject.

"What about you?" Lola asked. "You got a date?"

Danielle turned away from the suitcase and smiled mysteriously. The tactic had worked.

"You *do* have a date," Lola said. "Who is it? That Jeff guy from pottery?"

"No. Not the Jeff guy. Not even close."

"Who then?"

"Brent Gaynor," Danielle said.

"Wow," Lola said. "That's front-page news."

"Are you being sarcastic about Brent Gaynor?"

"No."

Danielle shrugged. "Well, he hasn't asked me in so many words. But I know he's going to. He's obsessed with me. He talks to me all the time now. He's always intercepting me at school, hanging around my locker, asking me all about this place."

Lola wondered who was intercepting whom. She didn't think she could stand to hear any more just now. Her head felt hot. She took off the flapper hat and tossed it on the bed.

"There's another thing, Lola. I've seen him sitting outside in his truck, right outside, looking up at this window."

She's getting worse, Lola thought. *A basketball star wouldn't be caught dead with a Wrigley girl. At least not in public, not in daylight.*

Danielle seemed to sense Lola's skepticism and pulled out her phone, ready with photographic proof. The big oak tree that stood just outside the bedroom window jutted into the picture, partly hiding the truck, but it was Brent Gaynor in the driver's seat all right, and just as Danielle had said, he was looking up at the building.

"It *is* him," Lola said.

"Of course it is," Danielle said. "You think I'm having hallucinations of Brent Gaynor?"

Lola skipped the evening meal. It seemed best to avoid Graham, Danielle, and the rest of the Wrigley Group Home residents. Besides, the voice that had encouraged her to buy the clothes had grown louder, and she needed some peace and quiet to hear what else it might have to say. This wasn't the kind of voice a crazy person hears, she assured herself, but a wisdom that seemed to come from deep inside her. It was a version of her own voice, and she trusted it.

On Monday morning, Lola was surprised to encounter Mrs. Dubois running the metal detector. The machine was beeping like mad while Dubois worked the sudoku.

"How come you're here?" Lola said as she passed through the machine.

"Oh, they're making me play cop today," Mrs. Dubois said. "Where've you been? I've been waiting for you in the library."

Lola stepped to one side and let the stream of students beep past. "Waiting for me? Why?"

"You signed on to clean up all that crap, but unless my eyes deceive me, the crap's still right where it was."

"That was a one-day thing," Lola said. She was about to add, *Go find yourself another slave,* but something stopped her.

Suddenly she wanted more than anything to return to that stinky, cozy reserve room. "I'm free right now," she said, although she had a midterm chemistry test.

"All right," Mrs. Dubois said. "Here's the key. Have fun."

Lola took the heavy old key. It felt good in her hand. She was halfway to the library when a page from the principal's office intercepted her.

"You Lola Lundy?" He was one of those freshmen whose voices were still trying to change.

"What of it?" Lola said. She couldn't stand for interruptions. Not now. That voice was talking to her again, softly, but it was there. And it wanted her to go to the library.

"Dr. Barton wants to see you ASAP," the kid said, and handed Lola a note saying as much.

"Who?"

"You know," the kid said. "Guidance counselor. Room 107."

Lola walked into the open door of Room 107 and there, behind a desk, drinking a cup of vending-machine coffee, was the turtle-neck man, still wearing the turtleneck. *The guidance counselor, of course*, Lola thought. Lola was disturbed to see that Hershey was with him. Hershey rarely visited the school. Something was up.

"Lola!" Hershey exclaimed, as if Lola were a long-lost friend encountered by accident. "How are you? Getting along all right?"

"Yeah. Everything's swell," Lola said.

"Swell. Well, that's retro," Dr. Barton said. He forced a chuckle that seemed calibrated to break the ice.

Hershey patted the seat on the couch next to her. Lola plopped down and braced herself for an annoying encounter; sitting down in a person's office never came to any good.

"How are you feeling today?" Hershey said. "I hope your migraine headache and ulcer haven't returned."

Lola smirked.

"I understand you've been volunteering in the library," she went on. "That's very positive."

Lola crossed her arms. "Thanks for the endorsement. What do you want?"

Dr. Barton and Hershey exchanged a glance, as if trying to decide who should talk first.

"Lola," Dr. Barton began. "I think it's best if we don't beat around the bush here. We have a report from the security company that you were trespassing on school grounds." He consulted a report on his desk. "Last week after the dance."

Lola had figured she'd got clean away with that. Graham hadn't checked the log. Danielle had kept quiet. Now here she was, blindsided by a delayed attack from an unexpected quarter. She tried to look placid, innocent. "You've got me confused with somebody."

"You were by the mermaid with your shoes off," Hershey said. "It was three-thirty in the morning, and you told the man you were washing your feet."

Lola felt her anger spike. There were spies everywhere, at every institution she'd ever been associated with, all of them waiting for the orphan girl to live up to her loser potential. And that guard had seemed more or less decent.

"I wasn't washing my feet," she said.

"Of course not," Dr. Barton said. "It's not even a fountain."

"It is a fountain," Lola objected. "The water comes out of the mermaid's mouth."

Dr. Barton raised the blinds behind him and pointed at the statue in the courtyard. "But the mermaid doesn't even have a head, Lola," he said. "See?"

"I mean, the mermaid did have a head once, and when she had a head, the water came out of her mouth. Look it up for yourself."

"You seem to be an expert on the history of our mermaid," Dr. Barton said. "For someone so new to the school."

"Like you said, I've been in the library a lot."

Hershey sprang from her chair. "Tell us what you were doing on school property at three-thirty in the morning."

"I fell asleep in the library," Lola said. "I did."

Dr. Barton cut in. "Let's all calm down. So, essentially, your story is you fell asleep in the library and when you came out it was night?"

"Yeah. Essentially, that's my story."

Dr. Barton referred to the report on his desk. "Would you like to talk it over?"

"No," Lola said.

The guard thought you were trying to break into the gym," Hershey said.

"I left my cap inside. So I tried the doors, but they were locked," Lola said. "That's all."

"When were you in the gym?" Dr. Barton asked.

"I went to the dance."

"Before or after you fell asleep?"

"Huh?" Lola said. She was beginning to lose track of the proceedings.

Hershey's eyes narrowed. "You went to a dance? You hate those things."

"I met some interesting new people, or old people, depending on how you look at it."

Dr. Barton made a covert notation.

"I don't believe you," Hershey said. She rose and took a few agitated paces around the office. "Were you running away again? You were running away and this guard interrupted you? Is that why you were outside so late, alone?"

Lola looked her in the eye. "No."

"I'm not hauling you out of another ditch in the middle of the night, Lola. I mean it. My bag of tricks is just about empty."

Lola stamped her foot. "Oh, for the love of cucumbers."

She hadn't intended to say it. It sounded bizarre. But there it was.

Dr. Barton grimaced. "What? Cucumbers?"

"I'm not running away. I like the house."

The adults let this sink in but looked skeptical. "Mrs. Graham must be awfully permissive," Hershey said. "What did she say about you coming in so late?"

"She didn't notice."

"I'll have to ask her about that."

"It might be better to ask her what happened on *Celebrity Cellulite*," Lola said. "She'll know that."

Hershey sat down abruptly and smoothed her skirt. She had no further questions.

"Can I leave now?" Lola said.

Seven

Dr. Barton and Mrs. Hershey watched as Lola disappeared into the corridor. Mrs. Hershey let out a deep breath and sank back on the couch. "She doesn't seem to be taking very good care of herself."

Dr. Barton examined the bags under Mrs. Hershey's eyes. "Neither are you. When was the last time you had a good night's sleep?"

"Her clothes weren't clean," Mrs. Hershey said.

"Weren't they?"

"No. And her hair wasn't combed. She's always been fairly neat in her appearance. And she seemed to be in a big hurry. Didn't you think so?"

Barton yanked at his turtleneck. "What does it mean?" he said.

Mrs. Hershey fidgeted with her purse and brought out a big plastic jar of antacid tablets. She popped two tablets and quickly chewed them. "It means she's up to something. You'll have to keep an eye on her," she said, licking her teeth. "I can't be in ten places at the same time."

Dr. Barton nodded. "I have tried. She's an elusive character."

"If she has her mother's illness, it's better we know now so we can arrange for treatment," Mrs. Hershey went on. "She's a nice girl, under all that armor. And smart, too, really sharp, although you'd never know it by her grades. I'd hate to see her end up living under a bridge, or dead. That's what so often happens."

Dr. Barton turned over the pages of Lola's Social Services file that Mrs. Hershey had placed on the desk in front of him.

"A criminal record, I see," he said.

"Nothing major," Mrs. Hershey said. "Some vandalism. A little shoplifting. Probably the worst thing she's done is hot-wire a car and drive it around for a couple hours."

"How did it happen with her mother?" he asked. "A teen mom, wasn't she?"

"Yes. Janine. She was seventeen, but she insisted on keeping Lola. Wouldn't even consider adoption. Wouldn't say who the father was. She dropped out of school and worked as a waitress here and there. Lived in the trailer park in Fairview. That's where she started to disintegrate. First she stopped going to work. Apparently she'd call in and say another waitress wanted to kill her or the cash register was reading her thoughts. That kind of thing. It seemed she started hearing voices around then, or seeing people who weren't there. Your classic schizophrenia symptoms."

Dr. Barton nodded.

"Then one day a truant officer found Lola wandering around in a park in the snow—she was about five—and when they investigated they saw the condition Janine was in. She'd nearly forgot she even had a daughter. They took her over to Hillside and put her on medicine."

Dr. Barton noticed a few students eavesdropping outside his office. He got up, glared at them, and shut the door. "What then?"

"Janine improved until she stopped taking the pills. A neighbor saw her in front of her trailer, planting capsules in a row in a tiny garden patch, very carefully, like they were seeds, and then watering them with a watering can and everything."

Dr. Barton stared into his coffee cup.

"In the end she was ringing doorbells around the trailer park and trying to collect donations in a cereal bowl, wearing only a bed sheet. She said she was an angel."

"And Lola?"

"Poor kid. She became a ward of the court then. That's when I came into the picture. I took Lola to her first foster home. She cried so hard the day we left the trailer. Janine was raving, incoherent, but Lola loved her anyway. She didn't understand why they couldn't stay together."

The bell rang. A herd of students stampeded by, changing classes, laughing and shouting. Then all was silent again. Mrs. Hershey chewed another antacid tablet.

"Go easy on those things," Dr. Barton said. "You'll get a kidney stone. So then what?"

"Well, Janine was in and out of Hillside for about a year, and once, when she was out—"

"That's when she jumped?"

"Right off the Jefferson County Bridge. There was one witness, an old guy who was fishing under the bridge. He said Janine was perched on a railing with a bunch of seagulls, and when the flock jumped, she jumped, too. He said she was wearing a white nightgown, and for a second or two she really seemed to be flying."

Dr. Barton brushed away a tear. He couldn't seem to develop the kind of protective shell Mrs. Hershey had. He often wondered if he'd chosen the right occupation.

"We moved Lola to the other end of the county. The idea was to get her away from the memories, the notoriety, to take her someplace fresh. That was about ten years ago. We'd never intended to bring her back, but we got cornered. Nobody would take a girl who'd run away so many times. The only place left was Wrigley."

Dr. Barton stared down at the papers in the file. "Was Lola asked how she felt about coming back here, to a place so full of bad associations?"

Mrs. Hershey looked uncomfortable, guilty. Dr. Barton had hit a sore spot. "We did sit down and talk it over," she said. "I was afraid of the effect it might have on her, coming to Ashfield.

But you know what? She said she doesn't remember living here. Doesn't remember it at all."

"Or doesn't think she does," Dr. Barton said. He closed Lola's file and handed it back to Mrs. Hershey.

"Thanks," she said, and stuffed it into her oversized purse. "I've got to go."

"Ever think about changing your line of work?" Dr. Barton said as Mrs. Hershey opened the door.

"Nah. This is it for me. Twelve more years and I'll get the gold watch."

"Social Services gives out gold watches?"

"That was a joke," she said, and was out the door.

Eight

Lola unlocked the reserve room and the familiar smell of mold and smoke met her nostrils. She climbed onto the *YOU SUCK* table and opened the window. A cold draft blew in. First she did away with an entire set of spongy encyclopedias, chucking them in alphabetical order into the bin with a barrage of good, loud *CLUNKS*. Then she went about gathering spines, covers, scraps, tables of contents, all mixed together on the boggy floor like some kind of word stew.

Hour after hour she read scraps of text as they passed through her hands and into the garbage: *At any time—one must be prepared—for the unexpected, the incredible—turn of events.* It hit her that a message was coming across in these bits and scraps, like an old-fashioned telegram; it was that voice again, the voice of her own subconscious, struggling to communicate. *Prepare yourself,* it seemed to be saying. *Prepare yourself because there is a way back. There is.*

An image flashed into her thoughts: It was her, tangled in a long, heavy rope like the kind used in tug-of-war. On one end was the present, and on the other the past that she had visited, and both were exerting a force on her. The present had won for now. But the pull was still there. She could feel it. Maybe there was hope. And if she found herself in that place again she'd hold on tight somehow, and not let go.

She paced up and down through the garbage for a long time, thinking the matter over. She tried to be sensible, practical. It came to her then that what she needed, what anyone in any time would need, was a home, a place to cling to. Where could she call home in 1923?

By the time the final bell rang, she knew. With planning, and a little careful subterfuge, she could make it work. She stuck her head out of the reserve room. The library was empty. Dubois had never come to check on her. Not once. She was beginning to like Dubois. School was just letting out when she jumped on her bike and pedaled back to the Yesterday Boutique.

Miss Bryant stood in the lobby, oiling the vintage cash register in the foyer of the defunct theater. She greeted Lola with a boiling-over of historical trivia.

"This cash register is older than the first bowl of Wheaties, yet eight years younger than the parking meter," she said, extending the oilcan. "Can you hold this a minute?"

She punched the *NO SALE* key and a loud *ding* burst from the machine. The newly oiled drawer flew open, and she slammed it shut with satisfaction. "Now then," she asked. "What can I do for you? A pair of dancing slippers, perhaps?"

"Not exactly," Lola said, handing back the oilcan. "I was thinking I'd like to know more about the Wrigleys. Since I live there and all. The history, I mean."

Miss Bryant's head snapped up so fast that her wig lurched forward over her eyebrows. At last she had found a young person interested in local history, a potential protégé. She had scarcely dared hope such a person existed.

She tore off the work apron that covered the familiar psyche-delic pantsuit, strode to the theater exhibit, moved the velvet rope aside, and beckoned Lola to join her in the salvaged seats. Side by side they sat in the exhibit, as if waiting for the house lights to dim, a screen to flicker on.

"Now then, what would you like to know?" Miss Bryant asked.

"Did they have any relatives? The Wrigleys, I mean."

"Cousins and such," Miss Bryant said. "Various. Rather spread out, I think."

"You mean far away?" This was promising. "Tell me about the faraway ones."

"Eunice Wrigley had a brother, an older brother. He went out west to join a mining operation. Maybe it was in Denver," Miss Bryant said. "But he wasn't heard from again. They figured the cholera epidemic got him."

"What's cholera?"

"A disease caused by bacteria in the water. Deadly bacteria. They couldn't cure it back then. Today, of course, with treatment—"

"What was his name?" Lola interrupted.

"Who?"

"Eunice Wrigley's brother."

Miss Bryant left her seat and headed into the theater. Lola expected another trip to the fruit drawer, but this time Miss Bryant angled down the slope. Lola followed.

A moment later the two were seated on the edge of the stage, their feet dangling into the orchestra pit, with Miss Bryant leafing through a volume she had dug out of a cardboard box. The book reminded Lola of the ones that had been ruined in the flood.

"Here it is," Miss Bryant said. "Waldron Larch Vance. Born in Ashfield County, January 18, 1887."

Lola leaned over her shoulder and took note of the spelling.

"The Wrigleys, didn't they like kids?" she asked, because this point worried her.

"My goodness, yes, they did. That's why they left their house to the county for youth programs. Didn't have any children to leave it to. Just couldn't have any. Who knows why."

Better and better, Lola thought. She nodded toward the orchestra pit. "Can I use one of those old typewriters down there? I could rent it. I'm interested in antique writing tools."

"Borrow one if you like," Miss Bryant said. "Free of charge from one historian to another."

Lola steered her bike with one hand and held the heavy typewriter with the other. Twice she lost her balance and almost crashed on the way home.

Lola was pleased to see that Danielle was out somewhere so she could work in private. If she finished fast enough she might avoid an interrogation about the strange machine she'd brought home and the stack of encyclopedias she'd borrowed from the common room downstairs.

She rolled a piece of paper into the machine, just like she'd seen people do in old movies, and hit a few keys. The letters came out faint but legible. It took Lola a while to get the hang of the thing, to get used to its loud *chonk* with each keystroke, the silly *ding* at the end of each line, and its maddening inability to erase. Apparently there was some kind of goo to cover mistakes, but Lola didn't have any of that so she proceeded slowly. The first several copies were a mess and went straight to the wastebasket. She marveled that the human race had once tolerated such clumsy, primitive gadgets.

By dinnertime Lola's letter was complete and she had returned the borrowed encyclopedias. She pulled the letter out of the machine and read it out loud to see how it sounded:

To my dear sister, Eunice,

Please take care of this poor orphan girl, Lola Lundy. She is the child of our distant cousin twice removed Horatio Vance Lundy, whom you must surely remember, and his second wife, Geraldine, God rest their souls, who were washed away when the Arkansas River flooded their lumberyard down in Pueblo two summers ago. Lola survived forty-eight hours alone in the loft of a neighbor's barn and has been in my care ever since. She is a good girl, polite and helpful, as well as extremely intelligent, but the mining camp has proved an unsuitable environment for a young lady of her caliber, as all sorts of ruffians and hobos are constantly hanging out, making trouble. A change of scene and perhaps a weekly pepperoni and onion pizza with extra pepperoni could do the child a world of good, I'd wager. I know that you will give her a good home and provide for the completion of her education, my dear sister, either in the bosom of your own home or with another respectable party. All is well here in Denver. We continue our mining operations, and by the grace of God our exasperating toil will bear fruit in the coming season.

Yours affectionately,
Waldron Larch Vance

Lola reread the letter and found it pleasingly authentic. She stuffed the typewriter under her bed. Then she decided she needed an envelope. You couldn't hand somebody a letter of such critical importance without an envelope. She raced to the drugstore on her bike and bought a box of envelopes. When she got back to the room she was unpleasantly surprised to find Danielle lying in bed staring at the wall. She wanted to address the envelope but didn't want her prying roommate to see the typewriter. Then she remembered, glory hallelujah, that it was Monday.

"Don't you have pottery tonight?" Lola asked.

Danielle's face looked even whiter than usual.

"Danielle?"

The girl didn't answer or even turn her head.

"You're going, right?" Lola demanded, picking up the digital clock from the nightstand and waving it in Danielle's face. "You'll be late if you don't get going."

"You'd like that, I bet," Danielle muttered. "So you and Brent Gaynor can be alone."

Lola took a step back. "What?"

"You heard me."

"Where'd you come up with that?" Lola set the clock back on the table and stared down at her roommate. Danielle was stiff with anger and almost as white as the sheet.

"So now you're gonna play all innocent," the girl hissed.

"I am all innocent," Lola protested.

"Brent Gaynor stopped me outside the Dairy Queen an hour ago and asked me what you thought of him. Like, what was your opinion of him. Like, do you think he's hot and all."

Lola laughed but instantly regretted it. To Danielle nothing about Brent Gaynor was a laughing matter.

"What? You think you're too good for him? So you're too good for Brent Gaynor, but he's all right for me?" she demanded, sitting up in bed.

"I'm not too good for Brent Gaynor. I just never thought of him at all."

"You and Brent Gaynor are totally checking each other out. That's the reason why he's been sucking up to me. He wants to get closer to you. How close has he been, Lola?"

"You're acting like an idiot," Lola said.

"I don't get you at all, Lola," Danielle went on blindly. "I thought we were friends. I help you get a job at Golden Recipe and then you do this."

"I haven't done anything."

"You did something. You must have done something to get his attention. This didn't all come from Brent Gaynor himself. Come to think of it, I still don't know where you were the night of the dance—you or Brent Gaynor."

"I was not with Brent Gaynor."

"You were," Danielle said. "God, I'm so blind. How did I not see it?"

"I have never been with Brent Gaynor," Lola said, pronouncing each word as clearly as she could. "I can't stand Brent Gaynor."

"There's a thin line between love and hate," Danielle quipped.

"That's crazy, Danielle."

Lola looked at the clock. She wished Danielle would shut up, get out of bed, and go to pottery.

"So I'm crazy? That's really funny. Everything you do is half-crazy, Lola. Everything you say is half-crazy. You don't see it. You talk to yourself and you dress up like a freak. I heard you were in the gym the other day doing some freak dance by yourself. Maybe that's what Brent Gaynor's into—the freak factor." Danielle smiled. "But I guess it isn't your fault. It must be in the blood."

"Shut your stupid mouth," Lola said, grabbing Danielle hard by the shoulders. The feel of the sharp bones just under the surface of Danielle's skin sent a wave of disgust through Lola. She let go of her and moved to the other side of the little room, as far away from Danielle as she could get. But the person she wanted to get away from was herself. How could she have been so stupid as to tell Danielle about her mother's illness and suicide? She jerked open her dresser drawers and started stuffing things into a duffle bag. "We're done," she said quietly.

"What's that mean?" Danielle shot back.

"I'm taking the empty room down the hall," Lola said. "You can notify Graham for me. And tell her why."

Danielle watched and chewed her fingers. "Lola, wait."

But Lola was furious, stung. "Watch out. Fingers have a lot of calories," she said. It felt so good right then to be mean.

"There aren't any blankets on that bed," Danielle whimpered.

Lola ignored her and cinched up the top of the duffle. Her hand was on the doorknob when Danielle began to sob.

"Don't leave me alone!" she screamed.

Then she was at Lola's side, clinging to her clothes, pulling her away from the door. "If you go, I don't think I can stand it."

Lola wriggled away, but Danielle pursued her.

"I was jealous. I am jealous. I've tried so hard to get Brent Gaynor to like me, but he just doesn't yet. And then you don't even try or even care and he's totally into you. But you can date him. I swear it. You can have him. I won't stand in your way. I'll help you, even."

Danielle was shaking now. Lola felt frightened by the outburst but still angry. She threw down the duffle. "Listen to me. Listen," she said.

Danielle took a few convulsive breaths and stopped crying.

"Brent Gaynor doesn't give a shit about you. He never has and never will. He cares about himself and basketball. Are you listening?"

Danielle nodded and sobbed.

"You have to stop thinking about him." She made her voice hard but was softening at the sight of Danielle's breakdown. "Think about something else."

Danielle went limp. "I will. I promise. It's over," she sobbed. "How could I like him now? I couldn't."

Lola sat down on her bed and stared at a chipped floor tile. "That thing you said, about how I'm half-crazy. I wish you hadn't said that. I wish you hadn't."

"I didn't mean it," Danielle said softly. "You aren't crazy. You're the sanest person here. You're my best friend. Not Beth. You. I'd never do anything to hurt you."

Lola looked at the clock. She had no time for a scene like this. She wanted to type her envelope.

She sat with Danielle a few minutes more, reciting all the worn-out slogans about friendship and forgiveness and healing she could remember. This was hard going, because Lola hated nothing so much as an inspirational motto: *Be all that you can be.*

Try, try again. Strangers are just friends we haven't met. She could just about vomit hearing stuff like that, or worse, seeing it embroidered on a pillow or stuck up on a poster in somebody's office. Before long, however, she had convinced Danielle that an evening at the pottery wheel was just what the doctor ordered; it would distract her from Brent Gaynor and help her forget their fight. Finally, Danielle stopped crying.

"Someday we'll look back on this and laugh, won't we, Lola?" she said, blowing her red nose. "Someday, when I live in an A-frame house on the beach in Florida with silk flowers on the table. And a white couch, one of those pit groups. And a big TV. And we'll be so tan."

"Yeah, we'll laugh someday," Lola lied. "And we'll be tan."

Finally, finally, Danielle left.

Lola watched from the window until her roommate boarded the bus, looking like a scarecrow in a sweatsuit. As soon as the bus disappeared around the corner Lola got out the typewriter and addressed and sealed her letter.

Voices in the front office woke her from a light doze sometime later. The letter was still clutched in her hand. Sound carried strangely in the old house, and Lola could often hear muffled conversations from Graham's office. But this was clear, loud, and angry. Lola opened the door and peered down the staircase. There stood the last person she expected to see, the last person she or probably anybody would have wanted to see: Mr. Terry. He was shouting at Graham in his curdled yellow voice.

"I insist on seeing her right now."

"It's after hours. And it's against the rules."

"You ignore my phone calls for days and now you're trying to blow me off. I came all the way over here," Terry said. "On my own gas money."

"I'm sure we can sort this thing out," Graham began.

"There's nothing to sort out. She stole my money. One hundred dollars. I'm prosecuting to the full extent of the law."

Lola had almost forgotten about the two fifty-dollar bills. The event seemed so distant, it was like somebody else had done it.

"And you've got proof of this accusation?" You could tell from the tone of her voice that Graham couldn't stand Terry either.

"You think I'd be here if I didn't have proof? You're not talking to some dumbo here. I have a master's degree."

Proof? Lola held her breath. What proof could he have? Fingerprints? A hidden-camera video? Or was he just bluffing? Probably the latter, but she couldn't count on it. She had to get out. Immediately.

"Look, Mr. Tracy."

"It's Terry. Gary Terry."

"Yeah. Mr. Gary. Calm down. It's pretty late," she heard Graham say. "Why don't we talk about this—"

"Don't tell me to calm down. Is she here? Is she upstairs?" Terry cut in, his voice getting louder, angrier.

"That's none of your business." Good old Graham.

"I might as well inform you that I've called the police," she heard Terry say, and as if on cue the front buzzer rang.

Lola rushed to the window. A squad car had indeed pulled up in front of the house. Terry must have some proof. She was in trouble. And she was trapped. She couldn't go out the front with Graham and Terry standing there. The back and side doors would trigger an alarm. All was lost, Lola thought, unless . . . She looked out the window again. The branches of the oak tree reached out toward the windowsill like two friendly arms. She had noticed the handy position of the tree before—the reflex of a girl who'd escaped from four foster homes. But were the branches strong enough this high up?

She could hear the voice of the policeman now and the three of them emerging from Graham's office. A set of footsteps sounded on the stairs, and then another, and another. All three of them were coming up.

Lola shouldered her knapsack and from under the bed yanked her suitcase from the Yesterday Boutique; she wouldn't leave her things behind for prying eyes. She held her breath and leaped.

Twigs attacked her on all sides. She heard the ripping of cloth and knew she'd torn her jeans. Rough bark scraped her palms. But her basketball treads expertly gripped the trunk. Even with the suitcase and knapsack the descent was easy enough, and in less than five minutes Lola was moving through the shadows of the neighborhood. Her thoughts turned to hiding places. The burned-out house by the library? That protected spot she'd once noticed under the Ashfield Trail Bridge? Then she hit on the perfect place, somewhere warm and dry and safe: the reserve room. It would do nicely, at least for the short term. She turned west, toward her destination. The fifteen blocks between the group home and Ashfield High lay deep in the hypnosis of television, video games, and computers. No one saw her.

The bank clock down the street was chiming eleven when Lola arrived at the borders of the campus. She hid behind a shaggy spruce across the street for a few minutes and looked for the night watchman. Finally, he appeared. It was that same traitorous slob who'd turned her in before. He was orbiting the grounds in a bored clockwise circle. As she watched, he sheered off to the parking lot. Soon she saw the flash of a cigarette lighter inside his car. He was smoking. Lola couldn't believe her good timing. She kept out of his line of sight as she raced onto the campus. She rounded the back of the building, passing the double gymnasium doors and the headless mermaid, and came up on the reserve room. The window was open, just as she had left it, and a low concrete wall boosted her up. The suitcase went in first, then the knapsack. She scrambled in after them over the sandstone facade.

Inside, it was velvety dark. Lola navigated by touch to the squeaky folding chair. She felt drained but triumphant. Nobody would ever find her here. Nobody came in the reserve room, not even Dubois, who was in charge of it. She wasn't sure Dubois could get in even if she wanted to. Lola still had the door key in her pocket. She placed her knapsack on the table for a pillow. Soon she was asleep.

Nine

She woke up. How close was it to dawn? For a while she sat in the dark and replayed the escape, felt the thrill of it again, and reveled in visions of Mr. Terry's face when she was discovered missing. She wondered if his eyes had bulged out when his sweet moment of revenge was denied him, and whether he had screamed in agony, or perhaps even suffered a mild stroke. But soon her mind turned back to the situation at hand, and she began to question the security of her hiding place. Would this be the day that the custodians decided to remove the damaged shelves? Hadn't Dubois mentioned they were slated for a trip to the dump? In any case, the custodians probably did show up early. Maybe some of the staff did, too, and those cheerleaders, to tape balloons to each other, or whatever it was they were always doing.

She ought to clear out, just to be on the safe side. Maybe she could return again the next night, but for now it was best to go.

She braced a foot on the bookshelf and hefted herself up to the window. The suitcase went out first, landing with a light scrape on the ground, followed by the knapsack. Lola hit the ground running. She scooped up the suitcase and raced into the windy fall night. She didn't bother to look for the guard. He could never have caught up with her or identified her in such darkness.

Soon she was free of the campus. She thought of Hershey. What would she say when she found out? The social worker's voice seemed to speak to her in the whine of the wind: *It's nearly too late, Lola. You'll be an adult sooner than you think. You have to pass these classes. What will you do without a high school diploma? What will you do?*

She stumbled and fell. Her hands landed in sharp gravel. She got up and looked around. Was she still facing the right way? It was too dark, the darkest dark she could remember. She doubled back, but after a few minutes the silhouette of Ashfield High reappeared. No direction seemed right.

She was tempted to sit down and wait for daylight, but then she remembered the guard. He might spot her, report her again—the dumbass—filling in his form with her name and the details of her odd behavior. She wondered if he would choose the same old tired adjectives: *disoriented*, for example, or *incoherent*. *Hostile* was a sure bet.

Again she tripped on something—a rock?—but this time was propelled into a tree. The impact knocked the wind out of her, but she was happy to find the tree. It was like an old friend, solid and reliable, or a buoy after a shipwreck. She clung to it. For an instant she saw the picture she must have made, a girl with an old suitcase, hugging a tree, in the dead of night. It looked crazy, unless you knew the context.

She couldn't just stand there and wait to be caught. She tried to think of other places she'd hidden before, in the dressing rooms of a public pool, or that slimy ditch. In one of her most desperate moments she had hid up at Eagle Rock Park. Eagle Rock was known for three things: drug dealers, illegal garbage dumping, and an infestation of large black rats. Even the craziest kids from the group home thought twice before going up there. Last winter, two people had been killed in a drive-by shooting in the middle of the parking lot in broad daylight.

A distant rumbling made her stop thinking and listen. The noise came from somewhere beyond the school, and it was getting louder. She crouched against the tree. It was a motor. A car was coming. A pair of headlights swept around the corner.

Lola watched the car pass, and never before had she seen such a contraption. It was rectangular and long, with dark blue paint, red spokes spinning on narrow tires, and headlights jutting out like a pair of old-fashioned spectacles. As the twin beams swept over the roadside, Lola confirmed that she was on Quarrier Street but saw that the long rows of townhouses were gone, replaced by an open field. She watched the car putter away into the dark.

Her head swam. She wanted to laugh, to scream, with joy. She steadied herself on the tree. She was back.

Graham and Hershey were no longer of any consequence to her. They were somewhere in the next millennium, along with the night watchman and Mr. Terry and her failing grades and everyone and everything else that had ever, ever bothered her in her entire life. It was all erased, everything, down to her own history. For at least ten minutes she stood, bathed in a kind of staggering euphoria, until finally the brisk air brought her back to the business at hand. The first thing to do was change clothes. She ducked behind the tree again and with trembling hands opened the old suitcase. Soon she was dressed head to toe in Yesterday Boutique merchandise, her regular clothes packed away.

She continued up the block toward where the Wrigley place should be, moving alongside what seemed to be a pasture. The light wind carried a pleasant scent that seemed so familiar. She took in a deep breath and then she recognized it, that same smoky mix of autumn leaves and acorns that clung to the pages of the yearbook. The dark was fading. Lola figured it must be nearly dawn. After about twenty minutes, she spotted the Wrigley house, first as a shadow, standing alone in a stretch of open land. Soon she could see the pale yellow of its bricks. The big house looked strange standing there alone, without the rest of the neighborhood packed around it, as if it had been cut out of a photograph with a pair of scissors and glued to an unfamiliar background.

With each step along the country road Lola found her euphoria turning into tension, and then fear. What was she doing, anyway? She stopped in the dust. She could turn around, but what was behind her? Where else could she go? At least in this direction lay a plan, however flimsy. She took a deep breath and kept going.

A heavy iron fence ran along the front of the property. She stood for a moment, looking through the bars. She touched the cold metal and felt intimidated. What kind of people, she wondered, built barriers like this? But she gathered her courage, pushed open the gate, and stepped onto the front walk. She recognized the heavy slabs of paving stone under her feet, and supposed they must have been too heavy for the county to uproot and replace with the kind of safe, dismal materials that had taken over the inside.

She tried out various opening lines as she moved toward the front door of dark carved wood, and had just settled on *How do you do?* when the rumble of an advancing motor made her wheel around. It was a truck, and it was headed in the direction of the house. *There's no reason to be afraid,* she told herself. *It's only a truck*—and then she fled in a panic across the Wrigley front lawn, slipping behind a corner of the house.

The truck stopped, and a man in a uniform got out. The police. Who else could it be? Someone in the house had mistaken her for a prowler. She had to run. But which way? She sized up the grounds. She could make a break for the meadow, with its cover of tall grass. Or was it smarter to climb a tree?

The policeman was almost at the door when she noticed that he was making a sound, like a rattling or tinkling. She took another look. He was carrying a basket of bottles. The milkman. He was only the milkman. Lola had heard of milkmen, of course, but this was the first real, live one she had ever seen. She watched him return to his truck and putter away.

She emerged from her hiding place, dusted herself off, and again inched toward the front door. She stationed herself next to the milk bottles but then couldn't decide: Should she ring the bell or use the brass knocker? Or just knock with her bare hand? As she stood struggling with the question, the front door swung open.

A man in a plaid bathrobe stared down at her through little round glasses. "My word. Have we got a new milkman?" he said. He was a robust person with a dark beard and mustache and graying hair parted in the middle.

"No, sir. I'm Lola Lundy."

"You're an early riser, Miss Lundy. What can I do for you?"

"Are you Judge Wrigley?"

"Yes."

"My name is Lola Lundy."

"So you've said."

"Oh, I did?" Lola said. She fished in the pocket of her dress and brought out the letter of introduction.

The judge took the letter. Lola watched him. What if Miss Bryant had misinformed her? What if Eunice Wrigley had no brother? What if he'd died ten years before her arrival at the Wrigleys' door and everybody knew it? What if he'd never gone to Denver but lived down the street?

The judge flung open the big front door and ushered Lola into the house. "Mrs. Wrigley," he called toward the staircase. "Come down, my dear. It's one of your kinfolk come to stay."

Lola heard footsteps in an upstairs hall, and then Mrs. Wrigley appeared. She was a pretty woman of about fifty with a lot of auburn hair piled on the top of her head. She ran down the stairs in a silvery-blue robe and matching slippers and took Lola's suitcase.

"Emmy-Faye from Detroit? But you're all grown up. Why didn't you write first? Don't tell me you've walked all the way here from the station. And in the dark."

The judge held out Lola's letter. "This isn't Emmy-Faye, my dear. This is Lola Lundy, come all the way from Denver, Colorado."

"Denver?" Eunice said. She took the letter and began to read. "Washed away in a flood? You must sit down, child. Henrietta! Caroline!"

Two uniformed maids appeared, one at the kitchen door and the other at the top of the stairs.

"Henrietta, set another place for breakfast. Caroline, make up the blue room, no, the yellow room. Cousin Lola has come to stay."

They ate in a sunny parlor with pink-and-white wallpaper facing the rose garden, a room that in the group home had stood up against the auto dealership and was used for storage.

Lola buttered her toast with a tiny silver knife and looked out the window. Paths of white stones meandered among several hundred rose bushes, the late-blooming varieties still brilliant yellows and pinks. Heavy trees in their fall colors lined the boundaries of the garden, and beyond, in the meadow, several horses grazed.

"We were surprised to hear from Wally after such a long while," the judge said. "Frankly, we thought something had happened to the old fellow."

"Wally?" said Lola.

"Waldron. My brother," Eunice said. "It is a comfort to me to have those few lines from him."

"Still in the mining game, is he? Stubborn so-and-so. You'd think he'd have given it up by now," the judge said. "He ought to come back. There's plenty of work right here in Ashfield."

"I know, dear. But when Wally puts his mind to something, he doesn't give up," Eunice said. "He's a very determined man."

"Especially with his physical limitations," the judge added, peeling his boiled egg. "He ought not to engage in such taxing work." The judge turned to Lola. "How's he doing with his ailment?"

"Well, he has good days and he has bad days," Lola said.

Both Wrigleys nodded knowingly.

"Do you hear that, dear?" Eunice said. "Good days and bad days. Let's send for him. Today."

"Blast, Mrs. Wrigley, you know the fool won't come," the judge said.

Eunice sniffed and her lower lip trembled.

"Oh, all right," the judge said. "I'll send a cable this afternoon."

The judge drew a small notebook and pencil from a pocket in his vest. "What's the address, Lola?"

"I don't think I can remember it," Lola said.

"It's too much travel. You're exhausted," Eunice said. "Let me show you your room."

Lola followed Eunice's trailing robe up a grand staircase, following a path she knew well but at the same time didn't know. They arrived at a door she did not recognize. Eunice opened it, revealing a yellow room flooded with morning light. In the center stood a large brass bed, plump with yellow quilts and pillows, and against one wall a polished mahogany chest of drawers and matching wardrobe. In a corner, near the fireplace, stood a rocking chair with a seat embroidered in blue morning glories. The stained drop ceiling was gone, and Lola looked up at a blue glass chandelier.

Lola struggled to get her bearings. It seemed that several of the dormitory rooms, including the one she shared with Danielle, must have been made by cutting up this one perfect room. Caroline had thrown open the windows to give the place an airing, and the long white curtains billowed at the windows. Lola soon realized that the difference in the light had to do with the absence of her escape tree. She glanced out the window and spotted it far below, just a sapling, barely taller than the rose bushes.

"Shall I unpack your things, Miss Lundy?" Caroline asked.

Lola noticed that Caroline had meddled in the suitcase. It lay open on the bed. A skirt sat on the top, concealing the yearbook that would not be published for a few more months but was antique-yellow and flaking with age.

"That's all right," Lola said, planting herself between the suitcase and the maid. "I'll do it."

In her concern over the suitcase, Lola didn't notice Eunice scrutinizing her clothes. Eunice reached out and felt the material of Lola's sleeve between thumb and forefinger.

"Your dress. It's the latest fashion, but it, pardon me for saying this, Lola, it looks so old. Even the buttons, they're faded, aren't they? Cracked, even."

Eunice was examining the whole dress now, from collar to hem. "What happened to this dress, Lola?"

Caroline, meanwhile, had reached around Lola and pulled the skirt from Lola's suitcase. Lola winced, then exhaled with relief. A blouse was still covering the yearbook.

"And this frock?" Caroline said, shaking out the skirt. "If I didn't know better I'd say it's been stuffed in a cedar chest for a good seventy-five years."

Caroline sniffed at the fabric. "It even smells a little mothy, don't it, Miss Eunice?"

"Caroline, please," Eunice said.

Lola laughed lightly. "Oh, this happens all the time out west. The sun is hotter, and the air is drier, and the wind is windier. And it's mothy. So mothy. Clothes don't last out west."

"Well, that's the first I've heard of it," Caroline said. "My sister lives out in San Francisco and she sent me her old wedding gown for my youngest girl and it was just good as new and—"

"Thank you, Caroline," Eunice said. "You may run Lola a bath now, and after she's had a rest, I'll take her shopping."

By evening, Lola had a closet and drawers full of new clothes, including two garter belts that she wasn't sure how to work, as well as two lipsticks and a box of loose powder with an oversized pink satin powder puff. Eunice had delighted in taking her up and down Main Street, from hat shop to dress shop to shoe shop, trying things on her like she was a doll. Lola felt so unlike herself, she was glad to have store mirrors to look into to confirm she hadn't changed into another person. The clothes, hats, shoes, and bags were beautiful, but her face was still her face. She wasn't, however, exactly herself. The Lola Lundy she knew could never have had a day like this.

Long, heavy cars, Packards and Nashes and Buicks of the sort Lola had seen in movies, were parked end to end all the way up and down the brick street, polished to car-show intensity, and the sidewalks were alive with dressed-up families on Sunday strolls.

"Why do you stare so, my dear?" Eunice had asked her as they moved through the crowd.

"Everyone's so dressed up," Lola said. "No jeans. No sweats."

"Different than the mining camp, isn't it?" Eunice answered. "But why should anyone sweat on a cool day like this? Oh, here's Mrs. Downing's shop. Let's stop in and look at hats."

It was the same Main Street Lola knew, and although the building facades were recognizable, she had to keep reminding herself she was still, somehow, in Ashfield. In the hat shop, Lola had tried on a dozen models before she noticed that this bright place with walls like a wedding cake was, in fact, that dingy pawnshop with the tarnished trumpets in the window. Later they passed the Grand Theater, no longer (or not yet) Miss Bryant's musty Yesterday Boutique but a social vortex, bright and blinking. A long line of people trailed away from the ticket booth, waiting to see a movie called *The Extra Girl*. In the crowd, Lola thought she recognized two of the musicians from the dance in the gym, but she couldn't be sure.

On the way home in the Wrigleys' big Hudson, Lola tried to get her bearings, but huge swaths of Ashfield, entire neighborhoods, were missing from this new, old landscape. On the east side of town, yellow grass stretched for miles to the flat horizon, where Lola believed a stinking paper factory would one day stand.

"Tomorrow we'll visit the high school. Would you like that?"

Lola thought of her lost necklace and of Peter, but not in that order. "I was a junior. I'd like to go back to school."

"Of course you would," Eunice said, patting her knee. "That's good thinking. A girl must finish her education. So many girls nowadays run off and get married without even a thought for graduation, much less college. Have you ever thought of college?"

"Not exactly," Lola said.

"You'll like Ashfield High. It's very modern. They have a wonderful chorus, and the Girl Reserves are quite active in town."

After a big roast beef dinner with the Wrigleys, Lola was overcome by a strange, intense drowsiness, yet she resisted sleep. Sleep had led her to this faraway place, and it stood to reason that it could just as easily carry her away again. But the feather bed pulled her in, deeper, deeper, until her worry yielded to a long, profound sleep in her second-floor room on Quarrier Street.

Ten

Eunice Wrigley drove Lola to Ashfield High on Monday morning, October 22, 1923, and walked her onto the campus. They passed the mermaid and her pool of wishing pennies, and Lola felt, despite the corny sound of it, lighter than air.

That morning she had awoken in the fluffy bed with a strange tingling through the middle of her, almost a burning, and she knew beyond any doubt that the tug-of-war had been won. She had been flung hard in one direction, slightly singed in the process, but the tangled rope was gone now. She missed no one, nothing, and went forward into the bright fall day of a new life.

She saw the students, so formal in their suits and dresses and long coats, chattering and laughing in little groups as they went into school. They looked so grown up, so enthusiastic, that she could hardly believe they were teenagers on the way to school on a Monday morning. But catching her reflection in the glass she could see that in her new clothes, hat, and T-strap shoes, she appeared just as grown up.

The principal set aside his morning business to attend to Mrs. Wrigley, one of the town's most prominent citizens, and soon the two had come up with a school schedule for Lola that included history, science, art, glee club, and home economics. When the bell rang, Lola found herself at a neat little wooden desk at the front of a history class. History was not her best subject; Lola would have been hard-pressed to say which subject was. The day's topic, announced on the blackboard, was the World War. What luck! Lola had seen a documentary about that very subject a few weeks before.

"For the love of cucumbers. Look who it is."

The high, familiar voice came from directly behind Lola's head. She turned, and there sat Whoopsie Whipple.

"Mike, is it you?"

"I guess it is," Lola said.

"Remember me?"

"You're Whoopsie. From the dance."

"That's right. Say, we thought maybe we'd see you around school last Monday, but then when you didn't come, we figured you thought we were all a bunch of big, dumb hicks and caught the first train back east."

"East?"

"To New York."

"Oh. Yeah."

Whoopsie punched Lola in the arm and laughed.

"Peter looked all over for you for a couple of days."

Lola leaned forward. "Peter?"

"Peter Hemmings. Mad scientist. The boy you danced with all night. Surely you haven't forgotten him?"

"He looked for me?"

"Oh my goodness, yes, and Paulette was livid. She could have chewed nails, I'll tell you that."

"Who's Paulette?"

"Why, Paulette Waters, the girl who's determined to become the designated Mrs. Peter Hemmings by graduation. Of course, he's too busy with his mad scientist routine to take much notice. But he sure did take notice of you, Mike."

Lola felt like she was hovering a few inches above her seat, like a helium balloon.

"You sure have changed in a week," Whoopsie went on. "You don't look anything like a boy now, Mike. Why, you're all cream puffs and sunlight."

"What were you saying, about Peter?"

Whoopsie ignored the question. "Notice anything different about me?" Her eyes were open wide, and her mouth hung open as she waited for Lola's answer. "Give up?" Whoopsie swept her left hand up from the desk and placed it close up in Lola's face. "I'm engaged. Thumbtack proposed right after the dance. It was your doing, Mike. Boy, was he jealous of that farmer."

"Engaged. Wow. How interesting. Have you thought this through?"

Whoopsie's right eyebrow arched up. "Huh? Thought what through?"

"You know. The commitment."

"What commitment?"

"Aren't you a little young to get married?"

Whoopsie laughed. "But Mike, I turned seventeen last week. I'm just the right age to be engaged."

"You are?" Lola said.

"Of course." Whoopsie waved the ring-hand. "Look. It's even bigger than Ruby Gadd's ring."

"Who?"

"Ruby Gadd." She lowered her voice. "Back there in the back row. She's been engaged to Hershel Vanderveen for six months."

"Congratulations, then," Lola said. "But what about that chorus girl stuff? Broadway and all?"

"Shhh. Not so loud. It's a secret, remember?"

"So Thumbtack's going with you?"

But Whoopsie didn't answer. Her face was a mask of studious alertness, focused on a spot at the front of the room.

"You there. New girl."

Lola twisted back toward the front. "Me?"

Miss Roach glared at Lola with small black eyes that sat on either side of a big knobby nose. Her black hair was pulled tight in a glossy bun. Lola shuddered.

"I shall repeat my question for the new girl, who was not paying attention," Miss Roach said. "Please explain the principle reason for the outbreak of the war."

Lola thought back to the documentary. It had actually been pretty interesting. "Hitler invaded Poland," she stated confidently. She was off to a good start.

"Pardon me?"

"That's right, isn't it?"

Miss Roach looked befuddled.

Lola changed course. "And the Japanese. They bombed Pearl Harbor and sank the USS *Arizona* and—"

Miss Roach's eye began to twitch.

"Wasn't it the *Arizona*? The *Arkansas*, then?"

Lola looked to the other students for support but found expressions of mild curiosity.

"Well, Miss—what's your name?"

"Lundy. Lola Lundy."

"Well, Miss Lundy. I don't know what type of schooling you've had in the Wild West, but here in Ashfield, we take our history seriously."

"But Hitler—"

"Who?"

She put a finger under her nose to simulate the notorious moustache. "You know. Adolf Hit—" Then it dawned on her: They must have been talking about World War I. Lola retracted her finger. Pearl Harbor wouldn't be bombed for another who knows how many years. Of World War I she knew nothing whatsoever. The truth be told, she could not even say with certainty who the participants were.

A boy in the back raised his hand and talked about colonial expansion and the assassination of an Austrian archduke. Miss Roach returned to her normal color. Lola shrank back into her seat and said nothing until the bell rang.

She hoped Peter might be in one of her classes or that he'd hear she was in school and seek her out. But when the final bell sounded she hadn't caught sight of him. Nor did she see him Tuesday or Wednesday. His absence seemed to inflame her imagination. On Wednesday night, she thought she saw him from her bedroom window, standing in the dark among the tangles of dormant rosebushes. But when she looked again, nobody was there. On Thursday she thought she'd spotted him at the far end of the east corridor, but he ducked into the chemistry lab. She began to wonder if he was avoiding her. Could it have anything to do with—what was her name?—that Paulette person?

At the end of school on Friday Lola positioned herself on the edge of the mermaid fountain and watched the students pour down the stairs. She pretended to be watching the cascade from the mermaid's mouth but was all the time looking clear through it, at the main entrance, determined to find Peter.

As the exodus trickled out, Lola felt she'd seen almost every other student in the school leave for the weekend, as well as most of the teachers. Now she began in earnest to wonder if Peter was avoiding her. He must have known she was attending classes. It was all over school. A new girl from New York and Colorado didn't show up in Ashfield every day. In fact, she'd been the object of great curiosity. Students had been approaching her all week with words of welcome, and even little presents. One girl had given her a lavender sachet, and another, a perfect apple.

When the sky clouded, she abandoned her vigil at the fountain and gathered up her things. The Wrigleys had offered to pick her up in the car, but she liked the walk past the brown autumn fields, and the feeling of arriving, chilly but clear-headed, at a warm home. The sidewalk came to an end a few blocks from the school, and she continued along the dusty shoulder, watching the clouds shift, revealing and then covering the sun, and the shadows that came and went under the nodding trees. She had ridden her bike up and down this same street many times but had never noticed the birdsong or the sound of the wind in the trees. Lola's old world had been cluttered and noisy, and had seemed to move so much faster. In this unfamiliar slowness, she noticed the last dandelions blooming along the ditches, the bark of a dog somewhere far off across the field, and the way the toes of her red leather shoes parted the dust.

She was halfway home when the squeal of tires made her look up.

"Hey! You! Mike!" Whoopsie Whipple beckoned from behind the wheel of a brand new antique Ford. Little Ruby Gadd sat in the passenger seat. "I'll drive you," Whoopsie called. "Get a wiggle on."

"Proceed at your own risk," squeaked Ruby. "She's not on the giggle water today, but you'd never know it by the way she drives."

Whoopsie punched the girl in the arm. "Oh dry up, Ruby Gadd."

Lola pulled open the heavy rear door and settled herself in the vast leathery living room of the back seat. Whoopsie hit the gas and the car rocketed down the road. Between the school and Lola's house, Whoopsie nearly crashed half a dozen times: a mailbox missed by an inch, a tree rearing up without warning, tires riding the rim of a rain-swollen ditch. Ruby shrieked all the way down the road. When a hunk of turf thudded against the windshield, she hurled herself into the back seat next to Lola.

"Whoopsie Whipple, you're not fit to operate an automobile," Ruby said.

"I'm not sure if it's any safer back here," Lola said as Whoopsie sideswiped a picket fence.

"That's a lousy place for a fence," complained Whoopsie, and honked her silly-sounding horn at it.

"You'll never see thirty, Whoopsie Whipple," Ruby said. "You might not see twenty."

The tires squealed horribly and then all was dead calm. Lola uncovered her eyes. The Ford was parked at the curb in front of the Wrigley house.

"Have yourself some dinner and then I'll be back to pick you up," Whoopsie said as Lola fled the car.

"Pick me up?" It was an alarming prospect.

"For the big sing at the Hillside home."

"Big sing?"

"I know it's only your first day in glee club, but you've just got to come, Lola. You'll add that certain air of New York sophistication to an otherwise gruesome event."

"Wear your crash helmet," Ruby called from the window as Whoopsie swerved back onto the road and out of sight.

The smell of baking met Lola's nose as she opened the front door, and Eunice's voice rang out from the sunny breakfast room. "Lola, is that you?"

"Yes, Mrs. Wrigley."

Lola found Eunice and the judge seated with a teapot and a tray of pastries in the back room, reading the mail.

"Have an éclair, dear," Eunice said. "And a cup of tea."

Eunice removed her reading glasses and looked at Lola. "Do you like the school? It's so modern, very up-to-date."

Lola nodded.

"Mr. Watson, the principal, you know, he made a few notes about your academic status for us."

Henrietta set an éclair in front of Lola and she took a big bite.

"You're a little behind, Lola."

"I'm *behind*?" said Lola.

Eunice patted her arm. "Now, you mustn't let that worry you. Understandably, your time among the miners has delayed your education."

Lola nodded sadly. "The miners. Yes. They did delay me."

"Of course they did, the damn filthy ruffians," the judge blustered.

"Lola, dear, the judge and I will tutor you," Eunice said, "and before you know it, you'll be right up-to-date. We know an intelligent young lady when we see one."

Lola wiped the chocolate from her mouth with a pretty embroidered napkin. "Thank you, Mrs. Wrigley, Judge Wrigley."

Eunice looked tenderly at Lola with her calm blue eyes. "I'd like you to call me 'Aunt Eunice,' Lola. If you don't mind."

"And you could call me 'Uncle Horace'; that is, if it sits right with you," the judge said.

"Could I?" Lola whispered.

"We're family, Lola. We'd be proud to have you call us your aunt and uncle."

Lola began to cry. The tears came up so fast that she didn't have a chance to stop them. It was how Eunice had said "family," and how she'd meant her, Lola. She'd never had an Aunt anybody or an Uncle anybody or an any anybody.

"Gadzooks, here come the waterworks. Just like your auntie here," Uncle Horace said, handing Lola his big white starched handkerchief. "Get it all out now, whatever it is, and you'll feel all the better for it."

"I'm all right, Uncle Horace," Lola said. "I'm fine."

"It's getting late. You ought to go freshen up for the glee club, dear. It's a fine community service they do."

Eleven

Hillside Manor was a big brick house, a local landmark, in fact, where Lola's mother had been taken time and again during the last year of her life. In Lola's time it stood at the center of a complex of modern glass-and-steel annexes: Wing A for old folks, Wing B for mental patients, and Wing C for the physically disabled, or, as she'd heard a fellow Wrigley resident once describe it after a brief, unhappy stay: A for *ancient*, B for *bonkers*, and C for *crippled*.

Now, as Lola looked up the wooded hillside, she saw only the original brick building and, from the talk around her, understood the place was an old folks' home. There was no parking lot, and Whoopsie left the car on the side of the road. Others girls were arriving at the same time, and small battalions of singers formed as the girls hiked up the hill, merging into a choir by the time they arrived at the big front doors and rang the bell.

Lola was surprised to see that the place didn't look at all like a hospital but rather like a great, big house. Persian rugs decorated floors of dark, polished wood. Heavy brocade draperies hung on the windows. The same sense of quiet that Lola had noticed everywhere pervaded Hillside Manor. No phones rang. There were no beeping machines, buzzing alarms, television chatter. The noises underneath that went unnoticed in Lola's day made themselves heard: the creak of a leather shoe on a plank, the rattle of a crystal doorknob, the soft knocking of a boiler, the jingle of a charm bracelet.

The audience was assembled in the main hall near the piano. The old ladies wore dark dresses that grazed the floor, and some sat in wheelchairs made of wicker. The old men had no teeth and smoked pipes and talked about the Civil War. Instead of nurses there were nuns, moving about in their long white robes topped with pale blue aprons.

The girls filed onto a raised platform and sang a program of folk songs, starting with "Foggy, Foggy Dew" and rolling right on through to "Mr. Rabbit"—Lola always a beat or two behind, trying to mouth the words. Afterward they stayed for tea with the audience. Ruby and Lola sat down with an old, old lady who described how she had buried her silver candlesticks to hide them from the Confederates and then couldn't find them again after the war.

The tea party broke up, and Lola went to get the coats from a cloakroom by the entrance. She was partway down the hall when she heard the ring of a hammer and glanced into the open door of a custodian's workshop. A man in overalls leaned over some sort of a machine, the parts spread around him on the floor.

Even from the back, she knew it was Peter. She took a step into the room. "Hello," she said softly.

Peter turned. At the sight of her he stepped backward, involuntarily, it seemed, and an expression like fear flashed across his face so fast that she wondered if she'd imagined it. "You're back," he said finally. "I'd heard."

She nodded. "I haven't seen you around."

Peter looked at her steadily but did not answer. His green eyes seemed to bore like an x-ray all the way through to her bones. He had not looked at her that way the night of the dance.

"I joined the glee club," she said. "We had a concert. And a t-t-tea party." Her teeth had chattered.

Peter pulled a rag from his pocket and rubbed slowly at the grease on his hands. He set the rag aside and reached into his shirt collar, drawing out Lola's necklace. "Here it is. Right next to my

heart." There was an edge to his voice. Of anger? Of wariness? Lola couldn't tell.

She realized with a twinge of guilt that she'd almost forgotten about her pretend heirloom, the fading fantasy of a twelve-year-old. "It's my—" She couldn't think of the word. She watched the gold chain graze the skin of Peter's neck and slide through his wavy brown hair as he pulled it over his head. He did not hand it to her but laid it on a work table in the middle of the room. He returned to his work, then, but she could feel him watching her as she went to the table.

The necklace was fixed and polished. She put it on. The metal felt hot as it settled against her chest. "I hope it wasn't any trouble," she said.

"It's what I like. Taking things apart, learning their secrets." Then he turned his back to her, as if their business was at an end.

What was wrong with him? His strangeness, his coldness, seemed to confirm that he had indeed been avoiding her. But why?

She glanced behind her at the open door. She wanted to turn and go through it but couldn't. She felt angry with herself. The old Lola wouldn't have stayed two seconds where she wasn't wanted. It was like she'd swallowed a magnet the night of the dance that kept pulling her toward Peter, making her seek him out in the pages of the yearbook and, now, in the flesh. She had been so sure that Peter liked her, that some strong feeling had passed between them.

"Do you work here?" she asked.

He didn't look up. "Odd jobs. Now and then."

She gestured at the metal parts. "What's all this?"

"An electric vacuum sweeper. Or it used to be. And I hope it will be again. Taking things apart is a lot easier than putting them back together."

"There's always duct tape," Lola said.

"Tape?"

"You know, it's that waterproof tape that—" she said, then caught herself; maybe duct tape hadn't been invented yet. Miss Bryant would have known, but she was somewhere in the future with the duct tape. She watched Peter continue to work. She could see that her presence unsettled him. His body was tense. Some powerful emotion was overtaking him, too. Maybe he felt the magnet, just as she did. Or was it something else? She thought again of that other girl Whoopsie had mentioned, that Paulette person who wanted to be Mrs. Hemmings.

The vacuum belt snapped into place.

Peter stood up.

He looked at her again, then moved toward her with sudden determination. He seemed taller than before. Instinct told her to back up, but she held her ground. He took her hand; he seemed to be feeling the bones, the joints, the texture of her skin, all the time looking straight into her eyes.

Lola noticed, more than ever, his beautiful face, the hard muscles of his arm. These were the same eyes she'd looked into at the dance, the same arms that had spun her in and out, but they now seemed to belong to someone else, someone older, frightening.

"I just wanted to see if—" he said, moving closer.

She felt paralyzed. "See if what?"

He ran a hand over her hair.

She could feel his breath on her face.

Neither heard the approach of Whoopsie, who swept into the room in a cloud of lilac perfume and stopped short, taking in the scene. Peter dropped Lola's hand and turned away from her.

"My oh my, what's this here? It's all sidelong glances and quickened palpitations." She opened her bag and took a swig from a little flask. "You must forgive me for bringing bootleg whiskey onto these esteemed premises, but the whole thing is just too, too gruesome." She collapsed onto a footstool, her legs stretched out in front of her. "No sooner do I pass through the front doors of

this joint than I start thinking about how one day I'll be a crotchety, withered-up crone myself. I'll have to wear false teeth and flat shoes and lug around an ear trumpet, and, oh dear, my hair, my beautiful curly hair. I can't bear it."

"You're only sixteen, Whoopsie," Peter said. He had returned to his task and was rummaging in his toolbox as if nothing had happened.

"That shows how much you know. I'm seventeen. I was seventeen last week. The Grim Reaper's stalking me." She offered up the flask. "Want some?"

They both declined.

Whoopsie screwed the cap back on and snapped the illicit liquor into her pocketbook. "Well, au revoir, Mr. Hemmings," she said, rising unsteadily from the stool. "Parting is such sweet sorrow, but Mike must take her leave." She took Lola's arm and reeled toward the door.

"Looks like I'm the designated driver," Lola told Whoopsie.

"Designated what?"

"I mean, you could get a DUI."

"A what?"

Lola changed her approach. "Can I drive your car?"

"You know how?"

"Sure. I drove all the time in New York."

She saw Peter's face darken as she pronounced the name of her fake hometown. He didn't believe it. What was he thinking? She looked down at the floor to make her confusion less conspicuous.

"Let's dash, then," Whoopsie said. "Ruby's waiting. Good luck with that contraption, Thomas Edison."

The three girls ran down the hill to the car. Whoopsie flung herself with tipsy abandon into the back seat, and Ruby settled into the front passenger seat, humming one last chorus of "Foggy, Foggy Dew."

Lola slipped into the driver's seat and found herself confronted with a set of controls as foreign as an alien vessel's. There were two metal arms flush under the steering wheel like the arms on a compass, a couple of mystery knobs down by her knees, a red-needled pressure gauge jutting up out of the dash in a threatening manner, and a weird little button under the steering wheel marked *START.* But where to start?

"Hmm," Lola said, rubbing her temples. "Golly ding. I think I've got a migraine coming on."

"Of course," Whoopsie said. "It's the old Hillside migraine. I get one every time I come over here. Thus, the hooch."

Ruby drove. Soon the Ford was skimming over the lonely roads back to town.

Lola stared out at the black trees in the dusk and watched drizzle snake down the glass. Her encounter with Peter had shaken her. She felt she'd waited a hundred years to meet him again, only to find him so different that it was as if a strange spirit had invaded his body. She had left him waiting at the fountain, yes, but could that account for such a change in attitude toward her? She felt it was something more, something to do with the way he'd felt her hand, and how he'd got close and touched her hair. Had he meant to kiss her? She didn't think so. It was more like he'd wanted to examine her up close, the way he'd been examining the machine on the floor. She couldn't forget his face, the tips of his fingers in her hair.

"Lola? Aren't you listening?" She realized then that Ruby Gadd was talking, and had been talking for some time, like background music you suddenly become aware of.

"Yes, I'm listening," Lola said.

Ruby was pointing out the window. "See right there? See? That's it."

In the dusk, Lola could just make out a construction site on the side of the road. "That's what?"

"I told you. It's my daddy's brick factory, or at least, that's where he's building it. They're just getting started on it—my daddy and my uncles."

Fairview, Lola thought. They were in that old dump Fairview, or rather, where that new old dump Fairview would one day stand, because now farmland and the occasional silhouette of a barn showed out the window.

The Gadd brick factory wasn't built yet, and she, Lola Lundy, knew how its crumbling carcass would look. People were forever trying to predict the future, calling hotlines and deciphering Mayan calendars, but being certain of it left her with an uneasy feeling, as if she'd just cheated on a test. She felt glad she stank at history; just imagine how much more of the future she might know if she'd bothered to study.

"You cannot imagine how fatigued I am of hearing about that blankety-blank brick factory," Whoopsie was groaning. "You might as well know, Mike, that's what passes for excitement around Ashfield. Well, let me tell you something: I'm gonna shake the dust of this one-cow hick town off my heels and see the world."

"Listen to the Queen of Sheba," Ruby said. "Shake the dust, my foot."

"Shows how much you know," Whoopsie said. "You just watch me and see what I do. I've got a plan. You just watch."

"And Thumbtack? Is he gonna shake the dust off his heels, too?"

"He'll come around."

Ruby turned to Lola. "Thumbtack Matthews is the biggest homebody anybody ever met. He wants to take over his daddy's mercantile as soon as he graduates, and this crazy flapper thinks she's gonna turn him into a city slicker. She's always showing him photographs out of those magazines of hers, but do you think he cares one hoot about New York? He doesn't. Not one hoot or honk."

Whoopsie crossed her arms and sulked. It seemed she couldn't argue the point. There was no denying that Thumbtack was an oak tree with roots anchored in the Ashfield soil. At last the car pulled up at the curb in front of the Wrigley house. The windows glowed yellow in the dark.

"Well, here you are, safe and sound—no thanks to me," Whoopsie said.

Lola threw open the massive car door. "I'll see you guys, then."

Whoopsie and Ruby shrieked like they'd been pinched. "Guys?" Ruby said.

"We say that," Lola explained. "In New York, I mean."

The girls nodded solemnly at the mention of that fabled city.

"All right, then," Whoopsie said. "See you, guy."

Lola was about to explain that two or more girls could be called guys, and that a guy in the singular was always a boy, but the whole thing seemed way too complicated. She stepped out onto the curb.

"Until tomorrow night, then, Mike," Whoopsie called after her.

Lola turned. "What's tomorrow night?"

"The picnic. You don't mean to say you don't know about it?"

Whoopsie had the same shocked look Lola had seen on Miss Roach's face the other day in history class when Lola couldn't name the sitting U.S. president. Lola had, out of politeness, hazarded a few guesses: Abraham Lincoln, John F. Kennedy, Thomas Jefferson, Winston Churchill, Paul Revere, General Custard, but the more she guessed, the more Miss Roach had twitched and clawed at her starched lace collar. Evidently it was some guy named Calvin Cartridge. Was it fair to expect a person to know a thing like that?

"Bring a big bowl of mashed potatoes," Whoopsie was shouting over the idling motor. "A big one."

"Wait a minute. What picnic?" called Lola.

"Up at Eagle Rock. The gang's having a bonfire."

"You don't mean Eagle Rock Park?" Lola said. "It's not very safe up there."

"You mean the bears?" Ruby called out, craning her neck around Whoopsie.

"Bears?" Lola said. "Are there bears?"

"They keep to themselves at this time of year," Ruby said.

"Real bears?"

"Well, we don't mean Teddy bears," Whoopsie called as the car slid away from the curb. "You poor, dumb New Yorker, you."

Bears at Eagle Rock sounded unlikely but plausible, like those stories on the news of crocodiles squeezing up pipes into people's toilets. But if nobody else was afraid, why should she be? And maybe she'd see Peter there. She had to see him again. She waved goodbye at the car and ran toward home.

Twelve

Thumbtack Matthews pulled up in his Nash Rambler late the next afternoon, with Whoopsie close beside him in the front seat. He was quick to jump out and open the door for Lola, and hold her covered dish as she got situated in the back beside Ruby and Hershel.

As instructed, Lola had brought a big ceramic bowl of mashed potatoes. Henrietta had stared at her for suggesting a Tupperware container, a thing unknown until 1946, and again, five minutes later, for suggesting that, instead of a dishtowel, the bowl be covered with Saran Wrap, a convenience unavailable until 1953.

The car smelled like fried chicken and potatoes and apple pie and old tobacco and Whoopsie's perfume. Thumbtack seemed to feel ridiculous for attacking Lola at the fall dance, and kept trying to atone for it with extra gallantry. The sun was setting as the Nash puttered up, up, up the hillside toward Eagle Rock Park. Lola knew the place well but was unable to recognize the curving country road they took to get there. It was a road long gone by her generation.

Coming over the hill, Lola saw that Eagle Rock's paved parking lot was gone, as were the familiar streetlights and the battered metal benches with their competing layers of graffiti. Thumbtack pulled onto a bumpy patch of hard-packed dirt where other kids had left their cars. Lola could make out several picnic tables not far from the fire pit, but beyond it stood the forest wall, heavy pines and bare November elms rising out of a thick undergrowth.

The bonfire was high and bright and threw cinders into the starry sky. Lola heard laughing and the strumming of a ukulele and smelled the sweet scent of pipe smoke she associated with old men on park benches.

Thumbtack and Hershel spread a picnic blanket smack in the middle of the action and unpacked the food: forty-eight chicken legs, four pies, an enormous meatloaf, a basket of buttermilk biscuits, a crock of butter, a bushel basket of apples, and half a dozen thermoses. There were hand-painted teacups and china plates, real silverware and linen napkins and little aluminum cups that popped up like telescopes out of little leather cases.

"Wow. Where'd you get all this food?" Lola marveled.

"Whaddaya mean where'd we get it?" Ruby said. "We cooked it, of course."

"All this? You made all this?"

"Well, it didn't fall out of the sky, Mike," Whoopsie said, biting into a chicken leg.

Ruby slapped a big slice of the meatloaf onto a china plate. "I'm almost too worn out to eat it now," she moaned, shoving a big forkful into her mouth.

"Very impressive," Lola said. "I would have ordered a pizza."

"What's that?" Ruby said.

"Ordered pizza."

"I mean, what's pizza?"

Lola looked at Ruby. "Did you say, 'What's pizza?'"

"Italian food, isn't it?" Ruby uncovered the mashed potatoes and jammed a big serving spoon into it.

"But everybody knows about pizza. Don't they?"

Ruby turned to the group on the next blanket. "Say, Virgil, what's pizza?"

"I dunno," Virgil said, and returned to his ham sandwich.

"See?" Ruby said. "This isn't New York. We don't have exotic foods or Italians."

"That's just one of the many problems with this one-cow, backwater hicktropolis," Whoopsie said, heaving a handful of acorns into the fire and watching them pop. "Everybody's just the same. We don't have any pizza food, and we all do the same things, on the same schedule, year after year, and . . ."

Whoopsie launched into her familiar sermon on the shortcomings of Ashfield, but Lola heard only the first sentence or two before her mind wandered its well-worn path back to Peter. She had examined every silhouette around the bonfire and found his missing. Maybe he wasn't coming to the picnic at all. The thought alone felt like some terrible piece of bad news. She wanted to ask about him but kept quiet.

On the other side of the fire, a girl began to sing along with the ukulele.

"I'm just wild about Harry, and Harry's wild about me."

Whoopsie got up and danced a little Charleston next to the picnic blanket and sang along: *"The heavenly blisses, of his kisses, fill me with ecstasy."*

Thumbtack watched her with an adoration that seemed almost religious. Hershel did a few card tricks for Ruby until he decided it was too dark.

Lola turned to Whoopsie. She had to work the conversation around to Peter but didn't want to be too obvious about it.

"I wonder if it'll rain," Lola said.

Whoopsie stopped dancing and plopped down beside her. "You mean you're wondering if Peter Hemmings is coming? You've been looking for him ever since we sat down."

It was no use trying to fool Whoopsie when it came to matters of the heart.

"If I know old Edison, he's over on the bluff with that telescope of his."

"You mean he's here?"

"Why? Wanna go see him?"

"I don't know. I didn't mean—"

"I know whatcha meant, Mike. Take the path over beside that clump of trees. When you come to the second fork, go left. Don't go right or you'll get lost on one of those deer tracks to nowhere. You'll come to the bluff above the swimming hole, and that's where Edison usually sets up. Here, take him some drumsticks. He's gotten too skinny."

Lola followed the dim path and in a few minutes made out Peter's silhouette on a bare, flat rock that extended over a ravine. He was alone, looking through his telescope. A crescent moon shone, reflecting down into the wavering black water of the swimming hole far below, and the sky was so crowded with stars that it looked to Lola like a science fiction backdrop. What had happened to the stars, she wondered, by the time her generation came along? Why had so many of them burned out? A rabbit skittered across the path at her approach and went crashing into the undergrowth. Peter turned toward the noise.

"Hello," she said softly, entering his camp. "Whoopsie thought you might be hungry." She set the bundle on a small folding table Peter had arranged near the telescope.

He thanked her with a pleasant, ordinary smile that surprised her after his strangeness at Hillside, and beckoned her over to his observation post.

"Does astronomy interest you?" he asked.

Was he again the friendly teenager in the man's suit she'd met at the dance? She began to wonder if she'd read too much into the encounter at Hillside. Maybe he'd just been mad at her for standing him up at the fountain. Her problem, she now saw, clear as day, was that she had spent way too much time dissecting every little conversation and event. Maybe he hadn't been avoiding her at all. Maybe he was busy with work, school, his family, who knows what? After all, did the whole world revolve around Lola Lundy? She almost laughed.

Peter lowered the telescope to Lola's eye level. She peered into the lens and the stars rushed in close. The moon was bright in her eye. Peter's nearness made her skin prickle. In the absolute quiet, she could almost hear the magnet inside her, buzzing, pulling her toward him.

"Enjoying good old Ashfield High?" he asked.

"I am," Lola said, and was surprised that she meant it; she did sort of love Ashfield. She loved a school.

"Making friends, I've noticed."

"Everybody's been nice. Strangers come up to me in the hall with little welcome presents. Like I'm a celebrity."

"There's a great deal of extra curiosity about you."

Lola wasn't sure if she liked that or not. "About me? Why?"

She heard him rummaging in some dry leaves with the toe of his boot.

"There are some pretty wild rumors going around about you."

Lola continued her exploration of the sky, no longer noticing anything she saw. "Like what?"

"Some of the kids are saying you're from Colorado, and that you lived in a remote mining camp so long you didn't know who the president of the United States was when you got here."

"They're saying that?"

"Funny, isn't it?"

Lola didn't answer. For all she knew, Eunice had shown her typewritten forgery at school. She better not deny it.

Peter reached out and made an adjustment to the telescope. She felt his arm brush her sleeve like an electric shock.

"I'd like to know more about you," he said, gently this time. "Real things."

She looked up at his face in the moonlight. The temptation to confess everything was almost irresistible. The secret, which had always been heavy, now seemed crushing. But she would not tell. No one could, or should, believe such a thing. And to say it out loud was to be a freak again, a notorious freak and outcast. She was done with that forever. "All right," she said mildly, turning her attention back to the telescope. "What would you like to know?"

The girl's singing voice came faintly across the heavy woods.

"The heavenly blisses
Of his kisses
Fill me with ecstasy.
He's sweet just like chocolate candy
Or like the honey from a bee. "

"I think you can guess."

His matter-of-fact tone startled her. It suggested he already knew everything. But he couldn't know.

"The vital statistics? Well, I'm five-foot-two and I weigh about a hundred and five pounds, I guess. My birthday's June the sixteenth. That makes me a Gemini, in case you're wondering."

Peter sighed, the way a teacher might when a student misses an easy question. He moved away from her, paced for a minute, then sat down on a boulder a few yards from where she still stood at the telescope.

"Hair, brown," Lola continued. "Eyes, blue."

"Blue-gray," Peter said. He folded his hands in his lap and looked up at her, as if he were gathering his thoughts. "Lola, do you remember the night of the dance?"

That evening, in fact, was recorded in her brain down to the last gesture. She could replay any scene in high definition, and had, time after time, during her many furtive excursions into the pages of the yearbook. "Yes," she said. "Of course I do."

"I waited around for you," he said. "At the fountain, until everybody was gone."

The moon seemed to grow brighter now, dusting Peter's hair and face in its pale glow. Lola felt drugged by the sight of him; he looked like something out of a myth in that light. *I waited, too,* she wanted to answer. *I waited hours and hours in the cold for you*. But instead she said, "I'm sorry. It got very late and—" She couldn't finish without lying, so she said nothing more.

"You told me you lived on Quarrier Street," Peter continued. The abrupt change of subject left her a beat behind.

"Yes, I did," she answered. "I do."

"I asked around for you on Quarrier Street the day after the dance and nobody knew you."

"I'd just moved in. That's why." She'd answered casually, but felt caught off-guard and tried to guess his intention.

"This is a small town," Peter said. "Everybody knows everything. But nobody knew about you."

"It was a mix-up," she said, trying for that same airy tone but not quite hitting it. "Why does it matter?"

"It matters because it bothers me, and it bothers me because I don't understand it."

Peter's voice was still friendly, but Lola heard a note of tension in it. He got up from the rock. She returned her attention to the telescope but knew he was watching her.

"So you're from New York?"

"That's right."

"Lola," he said. "Who's John Hylan?"

"John who?"

"John Francis Hylan."

"Am I supposed to know?"

"He's the mayor of New York. He's been the mayor of New York for the past six years."

She looked up from the telescope. An ambush. That's what this was. Peter was conducting one of those debunkings he'd talked about at the dance, and she, Lola Lundy, was its subject. Anger rose from the pit of her stomach.

Peter got up from the rock then and meandered over to the folding table. He unwrapped a chicken leg and took a bite, but he watched her, as if waiting to see how she would respond.

She was hot with shame. He had pretended to be interested in her, to want to "know more" about her, just so he could prove she was a fraud, some silly local girl who'd invented a glamorous biography for herself at a new school. How could she have walked right into it, she, who'd been subjected to that same interview technique dozens of times?

And there he stood, eating a drumstick, self-satisfied, thinking he knew everything about her when he knew nothing at all. She hated him.

"Congratulations," she said. "You can go tell everybody now what a fake I am. I don't have an aunt in France either, by the way."

"I figured that," Peter said.

"Tell anybody you want," Lola said. "Enjoy yourself. I don't care." She turned, shaking, and walked off in the direction of the bonfire. Disappointment and rage consumed her as she pushed forward in the dark over the rutted path, snagged by thorns, tripped by roots. The way seemed wrong. She had lost her bearings, and hesitated in a pitch-dark stretch hemmed in by leaning pines. A second path seemed to run off to the right. She took a step toward it, unsure, and in that instant, arms grabbed her from behind and she felt Peter's chest pressing against her back.

She opened her mouth to scream but didn't. For half a minute at least there was only his trembling breath on her neck, and then he began to whisper: "You're making me doubt my sanity," he said.

"Let go of me. Let go." For some reason she was whispering, too, when common sense told her she should scream.

"I know this is not the behavior of a gentleman," he went on, the words pouring from his lips into her ear like something hot and intoxicating. "But I don't sleep anymore. I can't think. There's no logic. Not since the dance. Not since . . ."

She could not understand him now. She had lost the thread, and was afraid. "I lied about myself. I admit it. I grew up right around here, right in this county. I'm not interesting at all. That rumor about Denver, it came from me, too. But you knew that. You've seen the letter, haven't you?"

"Yes. Very imaginative."

"What do you want from me, then? A public confession?"

"No. Not that."

She could hardly breathe in his grip. She knew at least half a dozen self-defense moves she normally employed with ample success in situations such as this, yet she was motionless. It was that magnet again, holding her against him. "What, then? What is it you want?"

"My mother always said too much study can cause a person to lose his wits," Peter whispered. "Now, you tell me, Miss Lundy. Have I lost my wits?"

He released her, then, and waited. She turned and ran for all she was worth, blindly. After a minute she stopped to listen for his footsteps but heard only the whine of wind in the pine boughs. He wasn't following her. She stayed still for a moment and waited for her heart to quit pounding in her throat. She squeezed her eyes shut and tried to make sense of the things Peter had said. His ambush had worked. He had uncovered her little lies about New York, and her half-truth about Quarrier Street, the nonsense about a French aunt and the mining camp. Her admission of guilt should have left him gloating, but it had brought on a frenzy. *You're making me doubt my sanity*, he'd said, as if feeling around the edges of the extraordinary truth.

There was one other possible explanation for Peter's behavior: that he was, simply, a perfect candidate for Wing-B-as-in-Bonkers of Hillside Manor. She wondered if, in the excitement of the dance, the bizarreness of the situation, she had not paid close enough attention to her elegant dance partner. She could usually spot a crazy kid coming a mile away, she who had moved among them for so long and knew all their tics and tricks. Had he sneaked in under her radar?

She opened her eyes again and found herself at a dead end. The songs and laughter of the picnickers that had come faintly through the trees during her encounter with Peter were now inaudible. She must have run a long way, but which way? It was cold, and so dark. Whoopsie's voice rang in her head: *Well, we don't mean Teddy bears.* Lola considered herself a survivor, and a reasonably resourceful person. She'd kept her wits about her during all sorts of situations. But her sense of direction had always been poor, and her knowledge of nature right around zero.

Then something flew into her face. She was sure it was a bat but afterward wondered if her own raw nerves had formed the creature out of a few dry leaves on a gust of wind. The next thing she knew she was being lifted, and voices were calling her name.

"It's all right, fellows. I've found her," boomed the voice of the person who was carrying her. It was Thumbtack.

In a moment, he brought her into the clearing where the bonfire was still burning, but lower now. A crowd gathered. Ruby chattered and fretted while Whoopsie fanned Lola with a linen napkin.

"Mike, you scared the dickens out of me," Whoopsie said. "A city slicker like you, alone with Mother Nature. It's not natural."

A few yards behind the others she saw Peter. The light from the bonfire flickered on his face as he calmly watched her.

"Where were you? Mike? What happened?"

She sat up. Her head was woozy.

"I got lost. It was so dark and something hit me—a bat, I think," Lola mumbled.

"A bat? For the love of cucumbers," Whoopsie said. "But I thought you were with Peter. Weren't you with Peter?"

"I couldn't find him," Lola said.

Peter withdrew from the firelight then, and moved off toward where the cars were parked. A moment later she heard the start of his motor and watched the dark form of his car disappear onto the country road sloping down from the park.

Thirteen

A month passed and then it was nearly Christmas. Ashfield glowed with colored bulbs, and the smell of fresh-cut pine garlands and hot cider floated over the downtown. Lola strolled Main Street between Eunice and the judge, looking into display windows that had become villages of toy trains and wind-up soldiers. Little by little, she was beginning to forget the Ashfield she had once known, its routes and houses and smells. She could not recall, sometimes, what had stood on this or that street corner, or the price of a Golden Recipe jumbo basket or the precise schedule of her days. Her old life seemed more and more remote, like a recurring bad dream that had finally left her in peace.

Peter had not approached her since their encounter at Eagle Rock. The stories about Lola's background as a New Yorker and a mining camp girl continued to circulate; he had not given her away. The thought of him made her furious, but she longed for a glimpse of him everywhere she went.

When Virgil Ludlow asked her to the Christmas dance, she hesitated and then cursed herself. The hesitation was for Peter, a person who had ambushed and exposed her. She accepted Virgil's invitation and went shopping with Eunice for the most beautiful dress she could find, a silk chiffon evening gown of midnight blue with metallic brocade and a low-cut back.

The only person who questioned her about her decision to go to the dance with Virgil was Whoopsie Whipple, on the day before the event, when she came over to bob Lola's hair.

"I'm gonna ask you flat out, Mike. Why aren't you going with Peter Hemmings?" she said, lining up her beauty tools on Lola's bureau.

"Was I supposed to?" Lola said. "Anyway, he didn't ask me."

"But you'd have gone with him, right?"

"No."

"But he's the one you love."

"No, he's not," Lola said. "As a matter of fact, I don't love anyone. And especially not him."

"Uh-huh," Whoopsie said, and chopped off Lola's ponytail. Lola gasped. Whoopsie dropped the hair and went right on talking. "I know true love when I see it. But then things ran off the rails somewhere. You wanna know what I think?"

"Not really."

Whoopsie snipped at the air. "You better change that to 'yes,' since I'm holding the scissors."

"Yes, then."

"I think something happened up there at Eagle Rock. The night of the bonfire. It was all sidelong glances and quickened palpitations up until then, and don't tell me it wasn't, Mike, because I'm not blind."

"He's wrong for me," Lola said.

"Did he get fresh?" Whoopsie continued.

"Not exactly." Lola said, although she wasn't sure what "getting fresh" entailed in 1923.

"Aha. So he did get fresh. I thought so," Whoopsie said, clipping away near Lola's ears. "How fresh, pray tell, did the man get?"

"I looked through his telescope and then he—"

"What? Then he what?"

"Whoopsie, is Peter like everyone else?"

"What's that mean? No, he's just like himself."

"I mean, does his brain work right?"

"Peter Hemmings's brain? Why, it's the best brain in the whole class, the whole state, I'll bet."

"Well, maybe not his brain, but his mind. Is his mind all right?"

Whoopsie put down the scissors and faced Lola, hands on hips. "Okay, what's eating you? What did he do out there in the woods?"

"Nothing."

"Nothing at all?" Whoopsie looked disappointed.

"I couldn't understand him. He wasn't making sense."

"Is that all?" Whoopsie went to work with a prickly hairbrush and some sort of glop from a glass jar. "Most of us can't follow half the things the professor says. He's a genius. But he's not a nut, if that's what you mean. Did he spook you with his moon-man talk?"

Lola groaned as the brush raked against her scalp. Nylon bristles were a thing of the future. "Maybe. Maybe he spooked me."

"You love him. That's what spooks you."

Whoopsie held out a mirror. Lola looked into it, and for a long moment she couldn't speak. It was no longer a kid, a teen, who looked back at her but a woman with sophisticated hair and beautiful clothes, a woman whose company people sought, and who was assumed by everyone to be good and sane and from a fine family. And it was also her, Lola Lundy.

"You're a living doll, Mike," Whoopsie said. "But careful you don't wear out my mirror."

Lola and Virgil rode to the dance in the back seat of Thumbtack's Nash, with Whoopsie in the passenger seat beside him. The night was cold with a light snow. Whoopsie shivered, opened her bag, and took a little nip from her flask. "Pardon me. I know this g-g-giggle water is destined for the Christmas punch, but I'm simply a g-g-glacier," she said.

Virgil held a heaping plate of gingerbread boys on his lap. They were still warm, and he smiled at Lola and rubbed his hands over them as if they were a campfire.

"Can you turn up the heat?" Lola called to the front seat. Despite her long fur coat, she, too, was shivering.

"Huh?" Thumbtack craned his red ear toward the back.

"The heat. Is it up all the way?"

"I don't get your lingo, city girl. You mean hit the gas?"

"I'm cold, I mean," Lola said. "It's ten-below back here."

"Still, I oughtn't drive too fast on this ice," he said.

Lola leaned over the seat and skimmed the instrument panel for the heat controls. There were none to be found. Cars, it seemed, didn't have heaters in 1923. Who would have guessed it? The car lurched on a patch of ice, flinging her back onto her seat. She pulled her coat tighter around her and hoped snow tires had been invented.

"Anyway, look," Thumbtack said. "We're here."

He parked at the end of a long line of cars. The teens of Ashfield, 1923, were passing through the courtyard in their finery, bright and beautiful, like ornaments against the snow. The foursome jumped out of the Nash and ran laughing and sliding for the gym. Through the flurries Lola noticed the bronze mermaid, presiding over a ring of ice.

On the stage a jazz band was playing.

"Five-foot-two,
Eyes of blue,
But, oh, what those five feet can do!
Has anybody seen my gal?"

The music sizzled and jumped like popcorn, and the wood floor vibrated with the slamming of leather soles. The gym had been decorated in silver and white, and glass stars dangled from the ceiling, flashing rainbows as they turned slowly on the currents of warm air that rose from the dancers.

A hundred kinds of Christmas cookies carpeted a refreshment table that ran half the length of the gym, and the smell of peppermint and cider flowed around the assembled bodies. Ostrich-plume headbands and sequined collars, fringed hems and silver shoe buckles, made everything glitter, flutter, twist, and float, an effect to outshine any disco ball.

"Turned-up nose,
Turned-down hose,
Yes sir, flapper, one of those.
Has anybody seen my gal?"

Lola and Virgil tossed themselves into the mix. Virgil was a slim, elfin-looking boy, popular and a good dancer, the best in school. Lola felt lucky to have him for a partner. A dozen other girls had been crushed when he'd asked Lola to the dance. She knew, now, what it was to be one of the most popular girls in school, embraced and admired and even envied, instead of the weird outsider best avoided.

After four or five numbers, Lola turned Virgil over to one of his many admirers and moved to the sidelines for a breather. She ladled some red Christmas punch into a cut-glass cup and wandered along the base of the stage, sipping and watching the band. There was a banjo player whose fingers moved faster than she believed human fingers could. It was the first time she'd ever seen anybody playing a banjo, the first time she'd seen a real banjo at all. A slow number began. Lola turned her attention to the saxophones, the clarinets, and tapped her feet along with them. The drummer smiled down at her and she waved.

When she turned back toward the dancers she saw Peter some twenty-five feet away, holding a girl in his arms. The punch cup dropped from her hand and smashed on the floor. She bent to pick up the shards, and in a moment Miss Roach was next to her, wiping up the spill with a tea towel and warning her not to cut herself.

Lola stood up. Her legs were rubbery. Why had she assumed Peter wouldn't be at the dance? It seemed ridiculous now that she had taken it for granted he wouldn't come without her. After all, what were they, really, to each other?

And that girl. Who the hell was that girl? Lola had noticed her around school. Peter was holding her close, and Lola could see that they were talking, confiding, smiling. *That must be Paulette Waters.* She was beautiful, with pale skin and thick auburn waves. Her teeth were white and straight as she smiled, and Peter, in a formal suit, was breathtaking. Had he given her the red rose that was pinned to her dress? Had he pinned it on for her? What was he saying to her? Could she feel his breath the way Lola had in the woods? At the memory of it she put a hand to her ear.

Then she saw Virgil. He was coming toward the refreshment table, flushed and euphoric. She turned her back on Peter and his date and poured Virgil some punch. As soon as he had gulped it down, she led him onto the dance floor.

The Ashfield High Christmas Ball of 1923 was cut short by a blizzard, but even so, Lola managed to dance with almost every boy in the room. Peter never approached her. He seemed not even to have noticed she was there.

Thumbtack's Nash skidded to the Wrigley house in the thickening flurries. Lola's heart sat like a hunk of lead in her chest. Virgil hummed scraps of songs as they drove along, tapping out the rhythm on his empty cookie plate.

The judge met Thumbtack's car in the drive, signaling like a railroad man with his lantern.

"Electricity's out," he shouted above the motor and the wind, as Virgil helped Lola from the car. "Not sure when we'll get it back in order." Snowflakes caught in his moustache and he sniffed.

Then Eunice leaned out the big front door. "Hurry, you two, before you freeze." She wore her favorite red velvet dressing gown and looked like a holly berry.

The judge rapped on the side of Thumbtack's car. "Better get these people home, Matthews."

Thumbtack saluted the judge, and Virgil jumped into the backseat and slammed himself in. The Nash fishtailed out of the drive. Whoopsie's gloved arm was still waving from the window as the car vanished into the snow. Lola took hold of the judge's arm and skated up the walk in her smooth-bottomed dancing shoes.

In the parlor the massive fireplace blazed, its reflected light capering among the glass bulbs of the Christmas tree in the corner. Oil lamps burned here and there. Lola thought the room looked like a fairy cave.

"Reminds me of the old days, by gum," the judge said, removing his gloves and slapping them against his thigh. "Things were simpler then. I almost miss them sometimes. Almost." Then he headed off to his study, saying he had some papers to read. He often consulted his law books until one or two in the morning, and seemed to require little sleep.

Eunice asked about the dance and Lola described the good parts—Virgil's dancing, the orchestra, the decorations, and the refreshment table.

"The whole thing was first-rate," she said. It was an expression the judge often used, and she had adopted it as a substitute for "cool," which everyone misunderstood as meaning unfriendly or dull. Lately she'd even uttered "swell" a few times.

"Caroline lit the fireplace in your room, and put extra blankets on your bed," Eunice said. "It should be nice and toasty by now. If you feel cold you must come and tell me." She gave Lola one of the oil lamps that was burning on the mantel, and together they climbed the big staircase, its banisters twined with fresh holly. Eunice kissed Lola on the forehead and went off down the hallway toward her bedroom in the east wing, her velvet hem brushing along the runner carpet. As fond as she was of Eunice, Lola was glad to be alone. The evening had been a trial. It had left her hollow and depressed, and the effort of concealing her feelings from everyone had exhausted her.

Fourteen

She entered her bedroom, the lamp lighting her way. Peter, still in his formal suit but dusted in snow, was asleep on her bed. He was half-reclined, his head leaning on the dark walnut headboard, his long legs stretched out in front of him on the quilt.

At the soft closing of the door he opened his eyes and looked at her. Neither spoke for a minute as the storm whistled in the eaves.

"You can call the judge," Peter said at last, his eyes never leaving her. "I'm sure he'd know what charges to bring against me. Although under the circumstances, he might just shoot me."

"How did you get in here?" she whispered.

"I climbed," Peter answered. He swung his feet onto the floor and began to brush the slush from his hair.

Lola moved to the window and looked out. She had estimated that long drop to the ground once before, the night she'd leaped out to her escape tree. Now her conclusion was the same; a fall from the window would be fatal. She closed the drapes and faced Peter. He was staring at her again. She felt lightheaded and steadied herself on the bedpost.

"Don't worry, I'm not dangerous," he said. "At least not yet."

"What do you want?" she said.

"I came to apologize."

"For which thing?"

"My behavior toward you."

"Including this latest?"

"All of it."

"You had to break into my house? You couldn't apologize at school? Or at the dance? I was there, you know. You were too busy with your girlfriend to notice."

Peter laughed, strangely, like he'd been tickled. It sounded to Lola like a crazy laugh.

"You mean Paulette?" he said.

Lola had been right, then. It was Paulette, Paulette Waters, the girl who intended to make herself Mrs. Hemmings by graduation. Despite herself, she was seething.

Footsteps approached along the hallway. Lola tensed and clapped her hand over her mouth; Peter sat quietly but composed, seeming not to care if he was discovered. The footsteps passed the door and continued toward the back stairs. It might have been Caroline or Henrietta, checking the fireplaces.

"I'll go in a minute," Peter said.

"How? Down those bricks? You'll break your neck."

"I don't care."

Lola took a step toward him. As he fell under the arc of her lamp, she noticed how thin he'd grown. There was a grim expression in his eyes that was new and disturbing. His palms were scraped and bleeding from his struggle up the bricks, and he was shivering. He was a shadow of the young man from the fall dance.

"Are you sick?" she asked.

"Yes," he said. "I have been for a while."

Lola felt a pang in her chest. It made her sit down on the bed next to Peter and take his hand. "What is it?" she asked.

He pulled his hand away and stood up. "I've been monstrous to you and I apologize. That's all I came for, to tell you that. I promise I'll stay away and won't bother you again."

Lola set her lamp on the bedside table. "Did I do something? Do you hate me? I'd like to know—"

"Can you accept my apology?" he interrupted. She heard grief in his voice, but resignation, too.

"Tell me what you have—what sickness," Lola stammered. She was lost again, fumbling in the dark to understand him, just as she had been at Hillside, and at Eagle Rock.

"It's irrelevant," he said.

"Please."

"It would embarrass us both."

"If you go without explaining, I'll never have peace. Why did you change?"

He walked over to the fireplace. He leaned on the mantelpiece and watched the flames.

"Do you remember the night of the dance?" he asked.

She nodded. It was the same question he had asked in the woods.

"We were at the mermaid," he continued. "And you said you were going to get your bag. Remember?"

"Of course."

"I was watching you walk away when it occurred to me that my manners had been atrocious. Not only had I mistaken you for a boy"—his eyes flitted over her chiffon-draped figure—"but I had neglected to offer to help you carry your books. So I went after you. I imagined you were going to the gymnasium, but you passed right through it into the school. That confounded me some, because you hadn't started attending Ashfield yet, or so I understood. Isn't that what you told me?"

Lola swallowed. He had followed her. How far?

He took a deep breath and resumed. "You ran along the hallway. I called your name, but there were still a lot of kids around, making a racket, and you didn't hear me. Then I saw you go in the library. Just as I got my head in the door, you were entering the reserve room. I followed you. Then I saw you. But—"

Lola tasted blood in her mouth and realized she had bit her lip. She could not imagine what he would say next.

125

"But I could see through you. You were like a ghost. I called your name, but you didn't hear me. The room was terrible. It was destroyed. Papers and books were scattered on the floor, and I smelled ashes. I called to you again and you dissolved like ashes yourself. Then the room was normal and I was standing in it, alone. I saw this as if it were real. I told no one, of course. I scoured texts, racked my brains, but I could not find any plausible theory to explain what I'd seen in the reserve room. Then you came back. You weren't a ghost; that much was obvious. You were solid as anybody, and besides, like I told you, I don't believe in ghosts or any of that bunkum."

"Peter. If you'll sit down a minute—" Lola began.

"Then the idea came into my head," he went on. "I can barely make myself repeat it now, out of shame—that you might be some kind of an alien being capable of dematerializing, and the more I thought about it, the more I believed it. I kept on watching you, from a distance, looking for a clue, a sign, to support this cracked theory of mine. I believed if I observed you for long enough, something would have to show. I watched you at school and a couple of times from down there, like a prowler." He gestured toward the rose garden.

"But then you appeared without any warning that night at Hillside Manor. And I couldn't help myself. I had to get close to you, see how you felt and smelled, and, I don't know, even what kind of a shadow you cast. But when I took your hand it was like any other girl's. That was more terrifying to me than if you'd had scales or horns; it meant that what I'd seen had nothing to do with you, that it had all come from my own mind. It meant that something was wrong with my mind, and if I couldn't trust my mind anymore, what would become of me? At Eagle Rock I tried again. I wanted to force you to tell me some secret that would prove to me that I was sane, but when you ran away, when you got lost and fainted, I saw myself for what I was, a madman who'd got stuck on a girl and then harmed her. I'd read of such men, of course, but I never—" He stared down at the rug. "I thought it would be enough to stay away from you, but when I saw you at the dance tonight, I could see you were unhappy and I knew it was my fault."

He stood in the firelight, quiet and spent.

"Stuck on me?" she whispered. She touched his cheek, and was surprised to feel tears.

"Well, what did you think?" he said.

He pulled her against him. His hands gripped her shoulder, her waist, her ribs, through the midnight blue silk.

"I love you," he said. She felt his warm lips on hers. "You are everything I ever wanted in the universe. You are my universe."

The room was spinning, and flashing with sparks, hail, meteors. Lola saw the image of the two of them, on a tidal wave of light, flying, racing through space.

"And you're mine," she said. It had been true since the first moment she'd seen him, or even before, when she'd only heard the sound of his voice in the gym, the night he'd thought she was a boy.

But he was already turning away. "I'm not someone you should love, or allow to love you," he said. "Believe me that I'm not. Trust me." His hand was on the doorknob. "I'll be absolutely silent. No one will ever know I was here. My parents are in Pittsburgh until Wednesday, so there'll be no questions from that end."

Cold formality had crept back into his voice. He had returned to Earth, and to everyday worries.

"There are things you don't know," Lola said. She took hold of his arm but he pulled away.

"Let me leave, Lola. For your sake. While I still can."

"Just wait," she said. "Wait." She was halfway across the room, reaching up onto a shelf, into a silver cup, for a hidden key. She unlocked the heavy cedar chest that sat against the footboard of her bed and began to toss out clothes and linens. Her hands were shaking. But there was no going back now. Whatever the consequences were, she would accept them, even if it meant being a misfit, a freak.

Peter stood, his hand still on the doorknob, watching the pile of garments grow. "What are you doing? Lola?"

"There's nothing wrong with you." She kept rummaging, unpacking. There seemed to be no end to the linens.

Peter crossed the room, dropped to his knees beside her, and took hold of her shoulders.

"Don't you see that I could be the ruin of you? I'm ill and I'll get worse."

Lola pulled away from him and reached back into the chest, tearing at the linens until she felt the canvas straps of her old knapsack. She yanked it from the chest and unzipped it.

The yearbook fell out onto the rug and opened to the page Lola had turned to the most, the senior class portraits from H to M.

"Look at it," she said.

Peter picked up the book. Lola watched his eyes move over the page. She heard his breath catch as he came to the photograph of himself in the oval frame.

He began to turn the pages, and stopped at the two-page spread on the 1924 Ashfield Senior Prom. "This is next spring." He held the book closer to the firelight and examined it. He was feeling the pages, becoming aware of the old paper, the frayed edges of the pages that were crumbling into his hands. He leaned into the book and smelled it. "How old is this annual?" he asked.

"Almost ninety years." Lola said.

He took her hand. His face was bright. "And how old are you, Lola?"

"I was sixteen. Now that I'm here it's harder to say."

They kissed in the firelight, and before long they were down deep in the feather bed, their party clothes falling away, lovers meeting in defiance of all the clocks and calendars. For both of them, it was where time began.

That night as they lay in each other's arms, she told him everything, about the ruined books and Mrs. Dubois, and about her life at the Wrigley house, split between the centuries. She showed him the pocket calendar she kept in her wallet. He was delighted with her plastic book-light, made in China.

His most urgent questions, on the mechanics of her movement through time, she could not begin to answer. She could say only that she had entered some kind of an unconscious state, something like sleep, and had found herself generations from her starting point, in the same spot, but in a different year. The first time, the night they had met, she had flickered between the two eras like a short circuit; but the second time, this time, the change had been permanent.

"I felt a cord fray inside me, and then break," she said. "I felt a pain somewhere around my heart. I knew then that I had been placed, or replaced in the time where I had always belonged."

Peter's analytical brain ticked all night with the implications of Lola's arrival. Could her actions now create ripples that would keep her from coming to 1923? But she was already in 1923. His mind jumped from one possibility to another.

"And this house, the Wrigley House. You have to make sure not to inherit it, Lola, or it'll never become a county home like you said, for you to come to live in, and, and then you might not come to Ashfield at all, or rather, have already come to Ashfield, but in the future, the future-past—I can see this needs a lot more study."

It was almost dawn when they locked the yearbook in the cedar chest. Lola, exhausted but wide-awake, drew back the drapes and looked out. The snow had stopped and a big moon hung in a sky bright with stars. She felt the first real peace she could ever remember. The secret was out, and impossible as it was, she had been believed. The feeling of separateness, strangeness, that had hung on her like a heavy coat all her life was gone. Peter joined her at the window and put his arms around her. Lola leaned against him. For a while they watched the sky.

"Is there life on the moon?" Peter asked sleepily.

"Nope," Lola answered.

"None? None at all?"

"None. Sorry."

"Are you sure?"

"It's just a rock. With no air."

"What do you mean, no air?"

"No atmosphere. You can't breathe up there. And you float."

"You don't mean to say you've been there?"

Lola laughed. "No. But a few people have. Astronauts. And they have to wear these special suits with air tanks on the back. I think it's cold up there, too, but I'm not sure how cold."

"Astronauts?" he whispered with awe. "But how do they get to the moon? Are there aeroplanes that can—"

Lola put her finger to her lips. Now Peter heard it, too, singing, coming from the east wing. It was the judge.

When I was young I used to wait,
On the boss, and give him his plate,
And pass the bottle when he got dry,
And brush away the blue-tail fly.

The house had begun to stir. Now they noticed, too, the distant clank of cooking pots. The judge's tune descended the staircase and trailed off somewhere in the vicinity of the breakfast room.

"He would shoot me, wouldn't he?" Peter said.

"Yeah," Lola answered.

Peter got himself dressed. He looked around for his shoes and found them by the fireplace. "Meet me later. Can you?" he whispered.

"If you make it out of this house alive."

"I'll pick you up. We can go to the Grand," he said, tying a shoelace. "There's a new picture tonight."

"What about the snow?"

"It's too warm for any more snow," he said. "At least it seems that way to me."

Peter left unseen by the garden door as Henrietta and Caroline argued in the kitchen, the judge worked in the front study, and Eunice took a bath. It was one of the shortest days of the year, and still purplish-dark out.

From her window, Lola watched Peter's shadow move through the fresh snow and away toward the field of winter cornstalks where he had stashed his car. She worried that someone might notice the footprints leading away from the house, but in less than an hour the north wind had blown them smooth as meringue.

Fifteen

That afternoon, Peter and Lola joined the line that snaked away from the ticket booth in front of the Grand Theater. The picture, much to Lola's surprise, was one she'd heard of: *The Sheik*, starring none other than Mr. Rudolph Valentino. She was going to get to see this Rudy in action. A photographer from the local newspaper walked up and down, taking pictures of the capacity crowd. A flashbulb popped in Lola's eyes.

"What about the rings of Saturn?" Peter was asking.

"What about them?" she asked, blinking.

"What are they made out of? How did they get there?"

Lola tried to remember. "They're millions of asteroids going around in a circle so fast they look like rings," she said. "At least I think so."

"You think so?"

"Sorry. We learned it in fifth grade. It was a long time ago."

The theater, just as Miss Bryant had claimed, was a showplace. Vivid murals along the walls depicted bears, wildcats, toucans, and camels, and were framed by twisting pillars washed in gold. A chandelier the size of a compact car gleamed with thousands of crystal teardrops in the center of a ceiling painted with clouds.

They took seats in the balcony. Lola knew the feel of the velvet seats, although the ones Miss Bryant had salvaged were squashed from decades of use. She settled back, holding Peter's warm hand. The theater seemed vast now, without all the junk Miss Bryant had crammed in there—Miss Bryant, who lived in the projection booth but wasn't even born yet.

As the lights dimmed, the blare of the Mighty Wurlitzer rose from the orchestra pit and Lola remembered like a pinprick the typewriter she had borrowed and would never return. But had she borrowed it yet? It was a question to baffle greater minds than hers, so she sat back and prepared to enjoy the show.

An organ in a movie theater seemed like an innovation to Lola, until the movie began and she discovered it had no sound apart from the live music. She had never seen a silent movie before, and the exaggerated gestures of the actors, the contortions of their faces, were hilarious to her. She laughed at the suspenseful parts that made the other spectators clench their teeth, and giggled at the primitive special effects. Valentino himself was a disappointment. The cheesy robes, the tweezed eyebrows, the lipstick, made him look more like a girl than the smoldering heartthrob he supposedly was. As Valentino burst into his desert tent, hands on hips, seducing some lady, Lola caught herself thinking about his funeral. He would be dead in less than three years, at the age of thirty-one, and she knew how and where it would happen. Miss Bryant had gone over the whole grisly end: the perforated ulcer in New York City, the galloping lung infection, the administering of last rites, the throng of thousands camped out under the window of his hospital room.

Sorry, Valentino, she whispered to herself under the strains of the theater organ. *I wish there was something I could do.* Peter seemed to sense her mood and put his arm around her. She snuggled into him, the man who knew her secrets, and felt the strange new peace of home.

The winter passed like a long but wonderful final exam in which any answer Lola could provide Peter was welcomed like the rarest of gems. She drew diagrams of cell phones and laptops, iPads and DVD players. They met whenever they could, often in Peter's workshop, a small converted horse barn next to his house, where he fixed things and worked on his inventions. They'd told Peter's parents, and the Wrigleys, that Peter was teaching Lola to read music and play the ukulele. And she was learning, at first to make it look good, and later, because she liked the instrument.

"What are we on today?" Lola asked, tuning up the ukulele. It was a beautiful spring day. The apple trees in the yard were covered in blossoms and their scent floated in through the open window.

"Mars," Peter said, pulling a fresh notebook and pencil from the drawer of a beat-up bureau where he kept all sorts of things. "Everything about Mars."

Lola played a chord. She'd learned three and could play her first song, "Little Brown Jug."

"Like what, exactly?"

"Let's start with the species that inhabit it."

Lola strummed a C chord. "There's no life on Mars."

Peter smacked his workbench. "Not even a plant? Not even one plant?"

"There's no water," Lola said.

Peter jotted it down: *Mars, no water, no life.*

Lola added vocals. *"Ha-ha-ha. You and me. Little brown jug, how I love thee."*

"What year will the astronauts go there?" Peter continued.

"Huh?" Lola said. She was searching the fingerboard for the next chord.

"The astronauts. What year will they go there?"

"They haven't gone yet. They've sent up a few robot things over the years."

Peter leaned forward. "Robot things? You don't say."

Lola nodded. "I do say."

"To do what?"

"Drive around and do experiments on the soil. *"Little brown jug, how I love thee."* What's this song about?"

Peter turned his notebook to a clean page. "Moonshine," he said.

"Moon shine. Now, that I'm not sure about," Lola said. "I think the sun reflects off the moon. Or the Earth shines on it."

"Moonshine is bootleg whiskey," Peter said. "That's what the song's about, some hillbillies who love their jug of moonshine. What kind of robots went to Mars?"

"Intelligent robots. With very intelligent brains."

"Not human brains?"

"Of course not. Whiskey's called moonshine? Why's that?"

"Because people make it in the woods at night, under the moon. It's illegal. Since Prohibition."

"Prohibition doesn't last, by the way." She strummed a G chord. "Only from 1920 until 1933. It was abolished under the 18th Amendment to the Constitution. I mean it will be."

Peter glanced at her and said nothing. Although he was eager to find out all he could about science, Lola's little bombshells on history seemed to shake him. When she'd told him about Valentino's death, the date, the place, the circumstances, he'd seemed spooked by it, by what else she might know.

"But these robot brains—" he began again.

"Humans built the brains and put them in the robots," Lola explained. "They're more like computers."

"How do the robots get up there?"

"Rockets."

"What kind of rockets?"

"I don't know. Space rockets."

"But you must know something more than that."

Lola shrugged.

Peter turned back a few pages. "All right. These satellites you mentioned. They do what, exactly?"

"I think they take pictures of stars and galaxies and stuff. And for television. And governments use them to spy on other governments."

"They spy? How?"

"Okay, so the satellite's orbiting the Earth and it has cameras that can take pictures of everything going on down below so you can see what your enemies are up to."

"You're saying the cameras up in space can see all the way down to the earth and make photographs? That's astounding."

"Yeah, I guess it is." Lola tried another verse of her song. *Me and my wife and a cross-eyed dog, tried to cross the river on a rotten log.*

"How do the pictures get back to the Earth?"

"Some kind of signals going back and forth between computers."

"What kind of signals?"

"I have no idea."

"All right. Now, what's this television?"

"It's a screen, like a movie screen, but it's small and you keep it in your house and watch things on it—like entertainment programs, movies, the news, or you can watch sports, listen to music, things like that. You can change the channels to watch whatever you want."

"There's sound?"

"Of course."

"That's why you thought Valentino was so funny?"

"If I moved my mouth and nothing came out, wouldn't you laugh?"

"I suppose I would," Peter said. "Anyway, how will it work, the television?"

"I have no idea."

"When was it invented?"

"Oh, a long time from now ago."

"Once upon a future past?"

"Or even sooner," Lola said. She set the ukulele aside. "I know what you're thinking."

Peter raised his eyebrows. "All right. What am I thinking?"

"You're thinking, of all the future girls, why did you end up with one who doesn't know anything about science?"

Peter tossed his notebook and pencil over his shoulder and gave her a long, long kiss.

"No. What I'm thinking is, if you hadn't come to me, I would have found you," he said. "Somehow I would have."

Once Peter had asked Lola about her parents. She'd told him she was an orphan, but he pressed forward and she had explained: Her mother had been young and alone. She'd gone crazy and jumped off a bridge.

"And your father?" Peter wanted to know.

"As far as I know, she never told anybody who he was. He was probably too embarrassing—some jackass—and she couldn't bear to admit it."

"Or maybe not. Did you ever think," Peter began, and then stopped.

"Did I ever think what?"

He turned back to his tinkering. He'd taken apart an old motorcycle for the heck of it.

"Go on," Lola said. "What were you going to say?"

"Well, that your parents were like us?"

"Like us, how?"

"Separated by time. But they weren't as lucky as us. And when she couldn't get back to him—"

Lola finished the thought. "She went crazy."

Peter had stopped tinkering and waited for her reaction. But she didn't answer right away. Her mind had never turned in that direction. If it was true, it was too sad to think about. She decided to forget it, to laugh at it. "Nah. It had to be some guy from school," she said. "Some nobody."

The seventeenth birthday of Judge Wrigley's beautiful niece from Denver and New York was a social occasion not to be missed. The rose garden was thrown open for the event, and all the dignitaries of town came bearing gifts. Mayor Wilfred appeared, and Clyde Meyers, Esq., the district attorney. Mr. Glidden, who owned the steel mill, stopped by with Mrs. Glidden and their little twin boys, as well as the entire Ashfield City Council and every neighbor within twenty miles. Mr. McCloud, the milkman, paid a call, along with Elvira Downing, with a gift from her shop, a blue chenille cloche hat with gold embroidery.

In a few hours, Lola received more gifts than she had in all her years combined: There was an Art Deco rhinestone choker, a pair of white deerskin gloves with a trio of nacreous buttons at the wrists, and another pair, net mesh for the opera, in silvery pink. There was a powder jar of pale yellow glass with a pineapple design on the lid, a string of hand-painted beads of Venetian glass, a sterling silver bookmark in the shape of an oak leaf, a Chinese green porcelain inkwell, a Spanish fan with an olive-wood handle, a tiny cellulose rouge box, a perfume atomizer of Marigold Carnival glass, and a glittering evening bag of rough-cut indigo glass beads with a push-button clasp in the shape of a flower.

Eunice had hired Mildred Longsworth to sit among the roses in a long white gown like a Greek goddess and play the harp, and the music, the perfume from the roses, the glint of the sunlight on her new gifts, the taste of lemon sponge cake, and Peter by her side, fresh from his graduation, made Lola feel that this day could never, even in many lifetimes, be surpassed.

But then Ruby Gadd arrived. She came darting into the garden with two other girls in tow, all of them overwrought and shouting for Lola. The party guests turned. The Greek goddess hit a wrong note. A man dropped his finger sandwich onto the walkway of white pebbles.

"It's Whoopsie," Ruby said, advancing, red-faced, up the lawn. "She's gone up the flagpole."

"What's that mean?" Lola whispered to Peter. She figured it was a piece of unfamiliar 1920s slang.

"I believe it means she's gone up the flagpole," Peter answered.

Ruby leaned on a trellis, out of breath.

"The flagpole?" said the judge, who had been enjoying a moment of peace on the davenport. "How the devil did she get herself up there?"

"She shimmied," Ruby said. "She's a great shimmier, it must be said."

Grumbling, the judge set aside his whiskey and soda and went to telephone the fire department, while the guests murmured about that crazy Whoopsie Whipple, who couldn't stay out of trouble.

"Thumbtack sent me to get you, to talk Whoopsie down. What you say carries a lot of weight with her, since you're from New York and all."

Peter coughed. "I'll drive," he said.

They rounded the block into Ashfield City Park, and sure enough, Whoopsie was atop the flagpole. The fire brigade men were busy extending a safety net around the base. Whoopsie might have looked like a sailor in a crow's nest had it not been for her new party dress of aubergine silk chiffon with lace inserts.

Thumbtack stood at the base of the flagpole, wringing his hands. His bow tie was askew.

Peter pulled up next to the fire truck and set the brake.

"Say something to her," Thumbtack shouted as his friends got out of the car. "She's out of her mind. She won't come down."

"What made her go up there?" Peter asked.

Thumbtack pulled a telegram from his pocket. "Just look at it."

Lola took the telegram and read:

Dear Miss Whipple, Congratulations! Your application to join our All-Cutie Chorus Line has been accepted. Please report to the Metropole Theater, Brooklyn, New York, before 1st August. Yours Truly, J.D. Fink, Impresario.

The chorus girl contest. Whoopsie hadn't mentioned it in months. With the hoopla surrounding her wedding, set for that fall, Lola figured she had exchanged her Broadway dream for another one. She returned the telegram to Thumbtack. He shoved it back in his pocket, walked a few tight, frustrated loops in the grass, and pointed a big finger up toward the flagpole.

"She wants me to come with her, but I can't drop everything at the mercantile and run off to Brooklyn, New York City. All-Cutie. I don't like the sound of that."

Mr. and Mrs. Whipple arrived on the scene just then and rushed the flagpole, their clothes flapping in a strong wind that was blowing up from the West.

"You're giving yourself sunstroke," Mr. Whipple bellowed over the wind. "You'll get sunstroke and kill yourself. And for what? For some fool notion about being a hootchy-kootch girl."

At the mention of mortal danger and hootchy-kootch girls, Whoopsie's mother jumped up and down and waved her arms. "Come down from there, you ungrateful brat. Come down."

The flagpole bent in the wind and Whoopsie clung to it with white fingers. "I won't," she said.

Lola approached the assembled officials and asked to borrow the bullhorn. The police captain was happy to surrender it.

"Hi, Whoopsie," Lola said.

Whoopsie waved. "Hello down there, Mike."

"Say something about New York," Ruby advised from the sidelines.

"Windy up there, isn't it?" shouted Lola.

"Sure is," Whoopsie called.

"I climbed a flagpole once. Girls used to climb flagpoles in New York all the time. I mean, back when it was in style."

The expected look of concern spread across Whoopsie's face. "Whaddya mean, *used to?*"

"It's out of style. At least in New York."

"Horsefeathers," she yelled. "I have to make some kind of a protest."

"I have some ideas," Lola said. "But I can't scream them at you through this thing."

The crowd watching Whoopsie grew. Families driving past pulled over and rolled down their car windows to gawk, and old ladies came out on the porches across the street.

"I wanna make something of myself, and now I've got my chance to be a big Broadway star, and are my nearest and dearest gonna back me? No. They want me to stay here like them because they haven't got a lick of ambition."

Civic attention was focused so tightly on the top of the flagpole that no one noticed the thundercloud bearing down from the West. Whoopsie was raving about the hick-town dust when, with a terrifying bang, a bolt of lightning struck the flagpole.

Several people screamed, Mrs. Whipple fainted, and Thumbtack reached up toward his stricken love. Whoopsie teetered for a second or two and then spiraled down, down, down. The firemen stretched their net to intercept the poor electrocuted girl, but Whoopsie landed on tiptoe and looked around as if she were surprised to find herself no longer upon her perch. Her clothes were charred and smoking, and her hair was standing on end, but she was undeniably alive.

"I've decided to come down," she said, smoothing her hair. Lola watched Thumbtack carry Whoopsie to his Nash and put her in the front seat, and saw the car move off in the direction of the

Whipple residence. Mrs. Whipple awoke from her faint and stood up. She was white yet fuming.

"Tomorrow we'll talk some sense into her," Mrs. Whipple said as she and Mr. Whipple started toward their car. "What she needs is a nice cup of tea and good night's sleep. Then tomorrow we'll talk through all this telegram business."

But by the next morning, Whoopsie was gone.

She had, as she'd always vowed, shaken the dust of Ashfield off her heels and headed for New York. Behind her she left all her friends, her parents, and her beloved engagement ring.

Sixteen

Lola snapped on her bathing cap and jumped off the bluff into the swimming hole. The splash sent a delicious shock all over her body, which had been perched on a rock, absorbing the August heat in wool swimming bloomers and a matching tunic. Peter was diving for treasure, and so far had brought up several pennies and a nickel. Now he burst to the surface in a spray of bright droplets, holding high a pair of steel-rimmed glasses.

"Hey, Matthews," he called. "Aren't these the spectacles Bob Gomez lost after the bonfire last fall?"

Thumbtack emitted a bored grunt from his post under a spindly sassafras tree, and relit his pipe.

"Well, I think they're Bob Gomez's," Peter shouted. He set the glasses on a boulder and dove again.

The three of them, along with Ruby and her fiancé, Hershel Vanderveen, had come up to Eagle Rock on a Sunday afternoon to escape the dust and heat of town, but the lush, heavy forest of August was almost worse; the trees seemed to exhale a sultry breath that clung to their skin and made them lazier than before. Only the swimming hole provided relief.

"Come on in. You can't just fry there like a big dumb catfish," Hershel called. "It's refreshing as anything."

Hershel kicked his long, white legs, sending up a cold spray in Thumbtack's direction. But Thumbtack didn't move. Since Whoopsie's departure more than a month before he had taken on the salient characteristic of his nickname: stubborn adherence to a specific spot. He sat and moped and wouldn't talk. He had refused to chase after Whoopsie. Not a single telegram or letter had he sent, such had been the blow to his pride.

But today, watching Thumbtack on the rock, Lola thought she saw a change in him. He seemed to be agitated, arguing with himself, and she wondered if the passing weeks were wearing down his resolve to let Whoopsie go without a fight.

"Come on in, Thumbtack," Hershel repeated, his head poking up from a clump of cattails. "It'll cheer you right up."

At this Thumbtack stood, rolled up his straw mat, and stomped away with his pipe clamped in his teeth.

"Hey!" shouted Hershel. "Don't go away mad."

"Not without lunch," Ruby added, calling from the picnic blanket where she had just set out five tin plates and cups.

But Thumbtack only tipped his hat and puffed up the hill toward his Nash.

"Let him go," Peter said. He had lifted himself out of the water and was reclined, sparkling and tan, on a rock. "He's got to figure this one out for himself."

After the swim, the foursome sat under a big shade tree and dug into ham sandwiches, deviled eggs, homemade pickles, and potato salad. Hershel had thought he might be able to get his hands on some beer but hadn't pulled it off, so they drank ice tea instead.

"Not a drop of anything interesting since Whoopsie left town," Hershel moaned. "Not a drop. Where was she getting it all, anyhow?"

"Oh, her daddy knew somebody who knew somebody else's daddy who knew a fellow in Pittsburgh," Ruby said, waving her pickle fork.

"Wish I knew somebody's daddy," Hershel said.

A beagle appeared, sniffing along the path, followed by an old man with two fishing rods and a bucket.

"Afternoon, folks," the man said. He was drenched in sweat, and his boots were caked with fresh mud. "Hey, ain't you the Hemmings boy? And you're one of the Vanderveens."

"Hershel, sir," Hershel said.

"Ah, yes. Of course," the man said.

Peter wiped the crumbs from his hands and stood up. "Hello, warden," he said, shaking the man's hand. "Fellows, this is Mr. Arthur, he's the fish and game warden up here."

"It's my day off today," Arthur said. He showed his empty bucket. "But fishing's no good."

The dog sniffed at the picnic blanket.

"Get out of there, Dandy," the warden said.

"Oh, that's all right," Ruby said. "Sit down here with us, why don't you? There's lots to eat, and we've got an extra place set, as one of our number has left in a huff."

"A huff, eh?" Arthur said, setting aside the bucket and adjusting himself on the blanket. "Well, gee, that's too bad. But lucky for me, I guess. In my view, a ham sandwich is always more satisfying than a huff in the long run." He noticed their bathing suits hanging on a tree. "Ya'll been watching out for the water moccasins in the swimming hole, I hope. They're vicious this year."

"What's a water moccasin?" Lola asked. She suspected it wasn't a type of shoe.

"Lola here is from New York City," Ruby explained as she gave the dog a bowl of water, "and retarded in the ways of nature."

"It's a kind of poisonous water snake," Peter explained. "But I've never seen one around here."

"What?" the warden said. "Last year Cletus Parker's dog was swimmin' in this hole and a water moccasin come up and bit him on the leg, and that old hound climbed out of the water and dropped down dead as a doornail."

"What a terrible story," Ruby said, fanning herself with her embroidered lace hanky.

"Cletus found that snake a day later and hacked its head off with a hoe," the warden added. "So, you see, the story's got a happy ending."

"That's the last time I go in that water," Ruby said. "But, oh applesauce, there isn't anywhere else to swim."

"There's always the Blue Hole," Peter said with a teasing smile.

"You can't swim in the Blue Hole. Everybody knows that," Hershel said, his mouth full of potato salad.

"What's the Blue Hole?" Lola asked.

"Swimmin' hole," the warden said, slapping at a mosquito that was trying to land on his neck. "'Bout a mile and a half up through the woods. But you oughtn't go."

"Snakes?" Lola guessed.

"Nothing that ordinary," Peter said. "Just that nobody's been able to find the bottom."

"It's more than that, Peter, and you know it." Ruby said. She turned to Lola: "People have disappeared up there. Not in recent years, but it's well documented that people have gone into the Blue Hole and never come out again. They fall in and get sucked all the way through to the other side of the Earth."

"That's all bunkum, of course," Peter said, taking a big bite of his sandwich. "Nobody's been able to get to the bottom of it, but there is a bottom, I promise you. If we had the right equipment—"

"Ya'll do yerself a favor and stay away from the Blue Hole," the warden interrupted. "Bunkum or no, there are places in this world that we don't understand, places where strange things take place and are best avoided."

Peter had reclined on the blanket, and was smiling that skeptic's smirk Lola knew so well, when he sat up abruptly.

"What's wrong?" Lola asked.

Peter dropped his sandwich and began to collect his things and Lola's. "We've got to dash," he said.

"Dash?" Ruby said. "But why?"

"Yeah," said Hershel. "The day's still young."

But Peter had already hefted his satchel. "Lola, remember the judge invited us for a game of dominoes? We're almost late."

In a moment they were in Peter's car, hurtling through the woods on a road of bubbling tar.

"Dominoes?" Lola shouted over the motor. "You hate dominoes."

Peter swung off the road into the gravel, raising a cloud of white, choking dust. "I've been so distracted. I've been so stupid," he began. "I've never been this stupid in all my life. I think you make me a little stupid."

"Thanks."

The forest breathed all around them like some huge, sleeping animal, and the cicadas buzzed and rattled in the heat. Peter stared at the dashboard.

"We have to destroy the school," he said.

"What?" Lola asked. She hoped "destroy the school" was a bit of slang that meant "go dancing" or "wash the car." But she could see from Peter's face he meant just what he'd said.

"Don't say things like that," she said.

"Maybe not the whole school," he muttered, half to himself. "But definitely the library. I suppose fire is the easiest way. Yes, fire."

"You're scaring me," Lola said, but he talked over her, his words running off like a lit fuse.

"You've always said you entered some unconscious state, that sleep, or something like it, was the common denominator of your movement through time."

"Yes," Lola said.

"You were asleep the first time you made the journey from your point of origin, and the second time, too, but you were wide awake when I saw you disappear in the reserve room."

"So?"

"It's that room. The reserve room. You fell through something in that room, a passageway, a gap, the way people fall through the Blue Hole to the other side of the Earth," he said, and couldn't help adding, "which, of course, is the greatest bunkum."

Lola shifted on the scalding seat. "But other people go into the reserve room all the time, don't they? And nothing happens to them," she said. "I've been in there a few times since I got here."

"Yes, but still, it's some formula that involves that room and you, the junction of the two things. The door isn't always open, but it exists. It's like a short circuit in time that pulls you one way or the other," he said. "It's as if time itself can't seem to decide where you belong."

"I know where I belong," Lola said.

She leaned over and kissed Peter. He kissed her back with a kind of desperation, and stroked her hair, still damp from the swimming hole.

"If you disappear again I think it'll kill me," he said. "I want to be with you forever. I want to marry you."

They kissed again in the hot car and she gripped him harder.

"But I won't disappear," she said. "I promise. We can get married and go far away. We can get on a train and go all the way to California and not ever come back to Ashfield."

Peter shook his head.

"As long as that doorway exists there is a chance that you will go through it," he said. "And this time, you might not be able to get back."

Not get back.

The words were like a shroud, suffocating her. They meant death. Because who would she be, back there? With each passing month, the old Lola had grown hazier, until now she could barely be remembered. She was like a friend who had died long ago, and whose concerns, dreams, routines, the new Lola had forgotten. She no longer existed, and could not exist again.

Peter's plan was simple. It involved a gasoline can, a box of matches, and the cover of darkness. Sentimentality toward his alma mater never entered the equation. The room must be destroyed, that was all. Lola went along, as the driver of the getaway car.

It was just after ten when they arrived at the school. Lola pulled into a gravel alley—long obliterated by her time—that ran behind the school, about fifty yards from the library window. She turned off the motor and got out. It was a humid, warm night without even the trace of a breeze. Everything was still except for the few crickets that chirped in the grass.

"This seems crazy," Lola said, looking up at the building. She found herself staring into the eyes of one of the gargoyles, which looked down at her with amusement as if it agreed.

"I know," Peter answered. He had left the car and was lifting the gasoline can from the back seat. "But I'm doing it anyway."

Lola caught a whiff of the gas and felt afraid. "Let's leave. Let's just leave," she begged.

"It's almost over," he said as he kissed her. "Wait here. Don't come in."

In a moment he was standing under the window. He lobbed a rock at it and smashed the glass on the first try. Then, standing on the low wall outside, he unlatched the window. In a moment, Lola could no longer see his dark figure. He had disappeared inside with the gasoline and matches.

Lola stood next to the car and kept watch, praying nobody would come upon the scene. A minute passed. After five minutes, Peter still had not reappeared. Then Lola saw a finger of smoke twirl from the reserve room window. The fire had started, but where was Peter? A cold fear came over her. She abandoned the car and in a moment was standing on the low wall herself, looking through the broken glass, a handkerchief over her mouth. She called Peter's name, but he didn't answer. Flames had engulfed the leather couch, and in their flickering light she thought, but couldn't be sure, that she saw a human form on the floor near the connecting door into the library.

"Peter! Peter!" she screamed, but there was no answer. Peter must have been overcome by fumes or smoke, Lola thought, or had been struck on the head, or had fallen. He would be burned alive if she didn't act.

She squirmed through the window, into the smoky room. "Peter!" She screamed, but the smoke was too thick.

Then she heard the sirens. The fire brigade. She hefted herself back up to the window and screamed out into the night. "Here! We're in here!"

She didn't care if she had to go to jail, she didn't care about anything but saving Peter. The door from the library opened and a man's silhouette appeared. It was dark, but even so, his shape seemed familiar. The uniform, the potbelly, the keys.

"Peter!" she screamed to the man. "He's in here. He'll be burned alive!"

"Burned?" the man said, looking past Lola into the reserve room. "What do you mean, burned?"

Lola whirled around to look behind her. There was no smoke. There was no fire. Just a dark room, and the smell of moldering paper. She cried out once more for Peter, and then everything went black.

Seventeen

Lola was dreaming about the Blue Hole. She stood on the rim and the water looked cool and welcoming. It was not an ordinary blue but the dazzling blue of a sapphire. The loose ground where she stood crumbled as she shifted her feet, and a few stones fell into the water with a plinking sound, headed down into the bottomless pit toward the other side of the world. She was watching the rings that floated out from where the stones had fallen when odd, high voices came from somewhere up in the sky. At first they sounded like birds, but then they gathered themselves into human voices. Lola opened her eyes. She was in a hospital room, and *The Simpsons* was on the television.

She sat up and looked around. In the next bed, a girl of fourteen or fifteen was eating a grape Popsicle. Lola closed her eyes again and begged to wake up, knowing she was already awake. A terror came over her, like the terror in a dream. She leaned over the bed rail and vomited.

"Hey. You're alive," the girl croaked cheerfully. "They wondered when you were going to wake up. Are you barfing? Gross."

Lola wished that her heart would stop, that her brain would burst, anything but this. She had believed that she was out of reach of her origins, that she had safely crossed a frontier as impenetrable as the one between life and afterlife. It had been months since she'd felt the cord that held her to her old life fray and then snap. She had been light as the wind, and free. But all that was an illusion. She had never been safe. The cord was still strong, and it had brought her back, just the way Peter said it could, through the reserve room.

"Hey. Didn't you hear me?"

It was the girl in the next bed. Lola turned now and looked at her, taking in the hospital gown, the messy red hair, the face full of freckles.

"What?" Lola said dully.

"I said," the girl continued, gesturing with her Popsicle stick. "They've all been wondering when you were going to wake up."

"Wondering?" Lola said. "Who was wondering?"

"The police, and a couple of ladies were here, too."

With the mention of the police, and the unnamed "ladies" waiting to question her, Lola felt the heavy return of her old self. It entered her body like a block of iron, crashing against her new one.

"The police?" she said, almost as a reflex. "When?"

"This morning. They said you stole money and broke into the school. I was pretending to be asleep and I heard them." The girl snickered with guilty glee. "Did you do it?"

"No," Lola said. "What day is it?"

"October thirtieth," the girl said.

"What year?"

The girl smiled, as if Lola was cracking a joke, but she answered the question.

Lola had been gone ten months, but it was the same night she had left. She had climbed down the tree only hours before, fallen asleep in the reserve room, and been caught without delay by the security guard.

She felt groggy and strange, as if she'd been given medicine. The cartoon voices penetrated her eardrums like sharp little forks and made it hard to think. She stood up. She felt it was time for urgent action, the nature of which she was still trying to grasp.

"I had my tonsils out," the girl said. "What's wrong with you? I saw the nurse give you a couple of shots."

"Shots?" Lola looked at her arms. Sure enough, there was a red spot on her right shoulder, and another on her forearm. *How dare they?* she thought. *How dare they?* She noticed she was wearing a hospital gown and a pair of thick socks that weren't hers. There were no bandages anywhere. Her arms and legs could move. It seemed incredible that she could still appear to be in one piece.

"Nothing's wrong with me. Must have fainted. Where are my clothes?"

"Dunno," said the girl. "Maybe they confiscated them."

Lola moved around the room, searching for her clothes. Standing up made her dizzy. She felt her head plunging toward the floor and grabbed the bed rail.

"You okay?" the girl asked. "You gonna puke again?"

Lola ignored her. She went to a basin beside the wall and splashed her face with cold water.

"Hey. You gonna make a run for it?" The girl seemed to be enjoying the sudden drama in her dull little hospital routine.

"What if I did run away?" Lola said. Her tongue felt thick.

"You'd be a fugitive. On the run from the law." She unwrapped her second Popsicle and looked Lola up and down. "I think you're about my size. You can take my clothes. But you better hurry."

"Where are they?" Lola said. She could almost hear the policemen's heels sounding along the corridor, just as she had heard them on the stairs at the Wrigley Group Home.

The girl pointed the Popsicle toward a locker near her bed. Lola moved to the locker and opened it. She found a pair of jeans, a sweater, and a red wool winter coat. There was a pair of galoshes, too. Lola put them on. The jeans were too short, but everything else more or less fit.

"You look great. Just like another me," the girl laughed. "Even the necklace. That *L* for *Liz*. That's my name. Liz."

Lola put a hand to her neck and felt the familiar *L*.

"Now. Down to business," Liz went on. "What should I say when the cops interrogate me? How 'bout if I say you were headed for Cincinnati, while meanwhile you go in the opposite direction. Chicago, maybe. Or Canada. That's it. The Canadian wilderness."

"Just tell them you woke up and I wasn't here."

"Play dumb. Gotcha."

"Thanks," Lola said. She reached up and took off the necklace, and handed it to the girl. She didn't need it anymore. It wasn't a real heirloom, and she'd received so much nice jewelry for her seventeenth birthday.

"You're giving me this?" Liz said. "But isn't it special for you? With the *L* and everything?"

"It's just something I found once."

"Thanks," Liz said, and started putting it on.

Lola opened the door a crack and looked both ways. There was no one. She turned back toward the girl and gave a thumbs-up that was conspiratorially returned, and then slipped out into the hall.

Lola noticed the stillness and realized that it must be the middle of the night. She got to the elevator and pressed the "down" button. There were three or four people in the lobby, staring sleepily at a television that was showing a commercial. She felt raw, conspicuous, glowing, but nobody noticed her as she walked out.

Eighteen

Danielle came back from pottery class, accompanied by her cousin Beth, to find her room full of people and a thrilling crisis under way. There was a policeman and a policewoman, Mrs. Hershey from the Social Services department, Mrs. Graham, and even Mr. Terry from Golden Recipe Fried Chicken.

"Where is she?" Mr. Terry sputtered at the girls as they came into the room. "You know. I know you know."

"Where's who?" Danielle said.

"Yeah, where's who?" Beth said.

"Where's who? Where's *who*?" Mr. Terry squealed. He turned imploringly to the police officers. "Are you listening to this?"

"Lola's missing," Mrs. Graham said bluntly.

"They all stick together, these gangster girls." Mr. Terry shouted, taking a step toward Danielle and Beth. "Now where is she?"

Mrs. Hershey went red in the face and imposed herself between Mr. Terry and the girls. "You've got no business here. I'm telling you for the last time. Get out. Get out or I'll cite you for trespassing. And I can do it, too, buddy."

Mr. Terry clenched his fists in fury. But the threat of a trespassing fine, on top of losing a hundred dollars plus at least four dollars in gas money, was too much for him. He huffed out of the room. "I've got my rights, too." His voice echoed in the stairwell as he stomped away. "You'll be hearing from me, or my appointed representative." The front door banged behind him.

A chilly wind was lifting the curtains.

Mrs. Hershey went over and shut the window. "Sit down, please, girls," she said.

Danielle and Beth nervously lowered themselves side by side onto Danielle's bed.

"Are we in trouble?" Beth whined.

"Not if you're honest with me. Do either of you girls know where Lola is?"

Danielle and Beth glanced at each other in alarm, then looked back at Mrs. Hershey and shook their heads.

"Try to think, Danielle," Mrs. Hershey continued. "Did Lola ever mention a hiding place, somewhere she might escape to?"

"No," Danielle said. "She's run away a lot, huh?"

Mrs. Hershey ignored the question. "What mood would you say Lola's been in lately?"

"Just her normal one. Quieter, maybe. She's got this old yearbook from the school and she spends all day staring at it. Hours and hours. If you ask me, it's creepy."

"A yearbook? A school annual, you mean?"

"A real old one. In black and white. With olden-days people."

"She stares at it? Do you know why?"

"She says she's interested in the clothes."

"The clothes?" Mrs. Hershey said. It didn't sound like Lola Lundy. She didn't believe it for a second. She turned to the two officers. "Finding anything else?"

"She was throwing away her homework," the policewoman said as she examined the contents of Lola's overflowing wastebasket. "Looks like a ton of unfinished assignments in here."

So far, the police had discovered two pieces of evidence—a wide-open window and a scrap of denim cloth fluttering on a tree branch just outside. From this they'd deduced Lola had heard the police on the stairs and fled down the tree.

Mrs. Hershey turned back to Danielle. "Did she maybe have a boyfriend somewhere?"

Danielle gasped, then slowly brought her hand up to her mouth. Although she had retracted her accusation concerning Lola and Brent Gaynor, the spark of suspicion had not gone out.

Her eyes darted back and forth. *Oh my God. Lola's on her way to Brent Gaynor. No, it's worse. She's already with him. They're in his car. She's telling him to run away with her. It's so obvious. That night she was out until four. That's when it started. Or before. And of course she lied to me. Liar. Lying pig. I've got to stop them. I could call his phone. I could call it right now, secretly, from the bathroom. But he changed the number last week and wouldn't give me the new one. I could try to find the new number. Maybe if I went to his house and searched his mailbox like I did that one time and—*

"Are you listening? Can you hear me? Danielle?" Mrs. Hershey was prodding Danielle on the shoulder. "What's wrong?"

"It's just the shock," Danielle said. "If anything happened to Lola . . . I can't even, like, think about it."

"Look at this. A strange letter," said the policewoman, who was still crouched over Lola's wastebasket.

Mrs. Hershey reached for the crumpled sheet of paper. She began to read silently.

To my dear sister, Eunice,

Please take care of this poor orphan girl, Lola Lundy. She is the child of our distant cousin twice removed Horatio Vance Lundy, whom you must surely remember, and his second wife, Geraldine, God rest their souls, who were washed away when the Arkansas River flooded their lumberyard down in Pueblo two summers ago . . .

The hair on the back of Mrs. Hershey's neck stood on end. She reached for her handbag and took out her Rolaids. She put two tablets in her mouth and chewed them as she read the rest of the letter.

"Hey, here's another strange letter. And another," Danielle said, rifling through her own wastebasket, hoping to reclaim her spot as expert witness. "And another. But they're all the same. Listen to this! A mining camp. In Colorado. Lola's never stepped foot out of Ohio. She told me so."

Beth let out a grunt-like laugh as Danielle waved the paper. "Four copies. She must have typed it over and over, the way crazy people do," Danielle said. "Like that maniac in *The Shining*. On that funny old machine she brought in today. She thought I didn't see the typing machine, but I did. She went out on her bike. That's when I saw it. She tried to hide it under her bed."

Mrs. Hershey plucked the copies out of Danielle's hands.

"Hey! Can't I keep just one?" Danielle pleaded. She had been imagining the look of gratitude on Brent Gaynor's face when she showed it to him. *Thank you, Danielle. You've saved me from making a terrible mistake. I've been so blind. It's been you all along. Not that fat, mentally insane Lola. I've been blind, blind, blind.*

"Of course you can't keep these letters. They're Lola's personal property, whether they're in the trash or not."

"But it's my trash can."

"I can't imagine why you'd want them. Unless you'd be cruel enough to show them to others."

Danielle began to cry. She had expected a much different response, a hushed thank-you, perhaps, for her teenage insight into crucial evidence. She felt cheated: first by Lola, out of her hard-earned right to Brent Gaynor's affections, and now by the Social Services department, which, come to think of it, might even owe her a monetary reward.

"I don't see what there is to cry about," Mrs. Hershey said. "Lola ran away from this chicken restaurant manager who accused her of stealing money. We don't know if there's any truth to the accusations, but she needs to face the matter head-on."

"It's just that, I didn't want to say, but," Danielle blubbered on, "but there's something else. Something so bad that I didn't want to say it."

Mrs. Hershey took a tissue out of her purse and handed it to Danielle. "Come on now. What could be so bad?"

Danielle covered her face in her hands, as if she couldn't bear to think about, much less say, what was in her head.

"Whatever it is, it doesn't have to go any further than this room. Would you like Beth to step out?"

"No. Beth should stay. She knows it, too."

Beth gazed at Danielle with her mouth hanging open. She had no idea what it was that she supposedly knew.

"All right then," Mrs. Hershey said. "I'm listening."

"It's about that fire in the reserve room. I saw Lola right before it happened, on that same night. We got in a little argument because she said she thought Ashfield High deserved to be burned to the ground. Of course I don't think so."

"Neither do I," Beth added helpfully. "Even though I don't go there."

Danielle held her hands miserably to her face. She opened her fingers a crack to gauge Mrs. Hershey's reaction. To her dismay, the social worker looked amused.

"I wish I had a dollar for every time I've heard somebody say they'd like to burn down the high school," she said, and turned to the officers. "Are we done here?"

"Wait," Danielle said.

Mrs. Hershey was getting impatient. It was late, and she still had several other matters to attend to. Things always seemed to go wrong at night. "Yes. What is it?"

Danielle sniffed pitifully. "Lola bragged about setting the fire. She said she volunteered to help clean the room so nobody would suspect her."

Danielle peeked through her fingers again and knew she had hit her mark.

"Do you realize what you're saying?" Mrs. Hershey said.

"Beth heard it, too," Danielle put in quickly.

Danielle and Mrs. Hershey focused their attention on Beth. It was the first time in Beth's life that anyone had hung on her words, and she paused for a long moment to enjoy the feeling.

"Uh-huh," she said finally. "She told us she set the fire. 'I set it' were her exact words, I believe." Beth was gaining momentum now, getting into the spirit of the lie. "She warned us not to tell anybody."

Mrs. Hershey sat down at the desk and stared blankly at the pile of papers that had come out of the wastebasket. She had known Lola for a long time and could have sworn she was incapable of such an act, or almost sworn.

"I'll get their statements," the policewoman said, taking over.

Mrs. Hershey nodded.

Nineteen

It was a cold night. What month had the girl said it was? October. Yes. October the thirtieth, still. The hospital stood on the edges of the old downtown, and Lola wandered into it. In a few minutes she entered Ashfield City Park and slumped onto one of the cannons. She knew it was not a good hiding place, but she needed a rest. Just a little rest. The cannon would help her get her bearings. It was solid and strong.

Sleet began to fall. She sat heavily with her eyes out of focus. But after a few minutes, she became conscious of the fact that she was looking straight at the facade of the Grand Theater. How desolate it was. Gone was the booth where she had lined up with Peter to buy tickets for *The Sheik*. She felt dreamy and strange.

An idea came to her; she stood up, removed the borrowed red coat, and draped it over the cannon. She took off the galoshes and then her hospital socks and placed them neatly on top of the coat. Now she was barefoot. She crossed the street to the Grand. She trod softly, and felt like some nocturnal animal rarely glimpsed by humans. A layer of ice had formed on the cement, but it did not concern her. She took her place in line for *The Sheik*—or rather, where the line had been. Then she could almost hear Peter's voice: *What about the rings of Saturn? What are they made out of?*

She smiled. Sleet flecked her face. She made no move to get out of the weather. In fact, she found herself willing the sleet to come down harder, for the temperatures to drop. The wisp of a plan had appeared in the park, a bold, stunning plan that was quickly developing into something magnificent: She would stay out in the weather until she died. She didn't feel sad about it. Not at all. Lola Lundy no longer existed anyway. She had existed once. She had lived with her Aunt Eunice and Uncle Horace. She was an important part of their family. She'd been loved by Peter Hemmings, and they'd planned to get married one day. She'd had friends who had sought her advice, a good standing in school, and a future she looked forward to. She had been given stylish gifts befitting a young lady of a certain social standing, and had been serenaded by a harpist. This shell that stood in the sleet did not contain Lola Lundy, did not contain anybody. It was like a fall leaf that should turn brown and fly off on the wind. It was nature's way. She was happy.

But soon a dog began to bark crazily somewhere nearby, and it made her think of the dog's owner. Someone might see her, standing there in line. They would return her to the hospital and try to cure her, try to make her look alive, when she was no more alive than a pressed flower in *The Ashfield County Herbarium.*

She moved into the alley to hide. There was a dumpster just behind the theater; she wedged herself between it and the brick wall. That lurching, floating sensation she'd felt in the hospital hung on her and made her clumsy. She did not see the two broken bicycles leaned against the side of the dumpster until she had knocked them over. The crash seemed like the loudest sound Lola had ever heard; she wondered if there was something wrong with her eardrums.

A moment later an alley door opened, and a rectangle of light appeared. Inside the light stood a figure in pink pajamas.

"Is someone out here?" came Miss Bryant's voice. The old lady took a couple of steps into the alley. "I see someone," she said. "Come out of there."

Lola left her hiding place. She stumbled over one of the downed bicycles and fell forward onto the wet pavement.

"Lola!" Miss Bryant shouted. "What's happened to you? Your feet are bare." She leaned over and placed a hand on Lola's back. Lola was still wearing the borrowed sweater, but it was frozen and soggy.

"Come in right now." Miss Bryant's voice seemed to come from the bottom of a well. She seized Lola's arms and pulled her up from the pavement.

A few minutes later Lola was in the projection booth, sitting limp as a ragdoll as Miss Bryant took away the wet clothes, dried Lola's hair with a towel, and dropped a heavy flannel nightshirt over her head. Lola did not resist as Miss Bryant lowered her head onto a feather pillow and tucked a comforter around her.

"Did someone do something to you?" Miss Bryant asked. "Should I call the police?"

"No. Don't. No one did anything. I was sick, but I left the hospital. I didn't want to be there, so I ran away."

Miss Bryant sat down in a rocking chair. Lola closed her eyes and listened to the creak of the runners. Her limbs ached and throbbed. They were thawing out. Like it or not, she was coming back to life, whoever she was.

"Why did you run away?" Miss Bryant asked.

Lola's eye sockets hurt as she focused on the old lady. "They think I stole money. They would have arrested me if I'd stayed there."

"Did you steal money?"

"I only stole it back. From someone who stole the equivalent from me."

Miss Bryant nodded.

"It was fair. More than fair. The police chased me and I ran away from Wrigley. I climbed out the window. Down a tree. I went to hide in the reserve room at the school. But then something happened in there."

"In the reserve room? What happened?"

"I can't tell you."

Miss Bryant scratched her wig thoughtfully. "It looks like you need to tell somebody. I'd listen."

"You'd think I was crazy."

"I doubt that. Give me a try."

Lola looked up into the thick spectacles. The eyes were large and luminous like heavenly bodies seen through the lens of a telescope. "I've been gone a long, long time," she said.

Miss Bryant got up from her chair. She sat down on the bed next to Lola and took her hand. "Go on. Whatever it is, I won't repeat it."

Lola knew then that she would tell Miss Bryant everything. What did it matter? The whole world could think she was crazy, crazy as her mother who planted pills in the garden and flew off with the birds, because soon she would fly off, too. She would make sure of it.

"I went to 1923."

"To where?"

"The year. I went to the year 1923."

Lola looked at Miss Bryant. Her mild, attentive expression had not changed, but she was nodding slightly. "Go on."

"I don't know how I did it, but I was there. I stayed for months and months. I lived with Judge Wrigley and Eunice Wrigley. And I fell in love with somebody. His name is Peter. He's nineteen now. We came to this theater and saw a movie, *The Sheik.*"

"Ah, Valentino," Miss Bryant murmured.

"Yes. But the theater was different. There were animals painted on the walls, in gold frames, lions, and one with a bear. The bear was catching a fish. And there was a toucan, too, with a big red berry in his mouth. He was in a tree, in a jungle. There was a chandelier, a giant one, with hundreds and hundreds of crystals on it. And there was a great big organ, with four keyboards, down in the orchestra pit. And a man played it. A bald man with baggy pants. I saw him."

"Just a minute," Miss Bryant said. She let go of Lola's hand and rose from the edge of the bed. "I want you to see something."

She left the projection booth. Lola heard the sound of rummaging in the balcony. Then Miss Bryant reappeared, holding a black-and-white photograph of the theater's interior. She handed it to Lola. "Is this your old friend the toucan?"

Lola began to laugh and cry at the same time. "Yes! There he is, eating the berry. And the grizzly bear. See, he's fishing, like I said. You can't tell from this picture, but the fish has a pink stripe, right down his side."

"Naturally. He's a rainbow trout, isn't he?" Miss Bryant moved to the other side of the projection booth and plugged in her electric kettle. "They painted over that mural in 1951. It was a shame. The new owners said they wanted something more modern."

"You believe me," Lola said.

"Yes, I do," Miss Bryant said.

"But how can you believe a story like that? I wouldn't have believed it unless it happened to me. Is it just because of the toucan?"

In her excitement, Lola had sat up in bed. Miss Bryant again helped lower her head back onto the pillow.

"No. No. It's simply, dear, because I know that such things do happen."

Lola was shocked. "They do?"

"Thousands of people disappear from this Earth every day. They don't die, or wash down a river. They just disappear, never to be seen again. Where do they all go? They slip through holes. It happened to my very own cousin in 1966. There are holes all over the place."

The kettle hissed. Miss Bryant poured out two mugs of tea and brought one to Lola.

"Holes in what?"

"I don't know if it has a name. I think of it as a membrane, with holes, or pores, that open and close. The skin of time."

Lola nodded and took a sip of her tea. It felt strange to be talking so rationally about something so irrational. For a second she wondered if she were asleep and dreaming the entire conversation, but the idea slipped from her mind as quickly as it had come.

"I'm certain," Miss Bryant said, "that there are several holes right here in the Grand. I might stumble into an open one someday and, zip, gone."

"What makes you think so?" Lola said. She took another sip of the tea. The drugs from the hospital were wearing off. It was easier to think.

Miss Bryant had sat back down and resumed her rocking. "At night, sometimes, when I'm sleeping up here in the projection booth, I hear the click of the film running through the projector, and sometimes I hear the organ, too, down there in the pit, just faintly. I hear the audience now and again, too, laughing or gasping or clapping. And I know they aren't ghosts."

"Ghosts are all bunkum," Lola added.

"Decidedly," Miss Bryant said. "What I hear are live people, alive as I am, out of reach but close at the same time."

"Like trains, maybe" Lola said. "Running along parallel tracks."

"Yes. Just like that. Passing close enough so the passengers might see one another through the lighted windows. Sometimes, I wonder how it would be to make a mad leap, like in an action film, and land on the roof of the other train, and make one's way in, and sit down among the passengers, and then continue along on that other train."

"The hole I fell through, I know where it is. It's in the reserve room of the Ashfield High School library. It goes to 1923. But it isn't always open."

"See, that's just what I mean," Miss Bryant said. "It's all there, just beyond the membrane."

Lola had finished her tea. Miss Bryant took away the cup.

"You have to sleep now," she said, giving Lola a pat on the head. "Try not to think about anything for a while."

Miss Bryant unplugged the kettle, turned off the light, and went out. Lola heard her footsteps fading down the track that twisted through the heaped balcony.

In the night Lola had strange, vivid dreams and heard voices: *Change the reel, Floyd. Floyd! Put out that cigarette right this minute and change the reel. Buzz off, why don't you, Elmer. Go on and mind your own beeswax.* And then the flick-flick-flick-flick-flick of film slapping against itself, the buzz of a crowd, the lurching chords of a theater organ.

Twenty

By the time the police finished taking the girls' statements, it was very late. Beth got to go home in a squad car. Danielle tossed and turned with fevered visions of Brent Gaynor until sleep overtook her.

She awoke early and took a bus across town, then walked six blocks to the tree-lined street where Brent Gaynor lived. She stood hidden in a bush for two tense hours until Brent Gaynor appeared, alone, in his driveway, dressed for basketball practice, and drove away in his truck. All was well. Brent had not eloped with Lola. Danielle felt giddy. She skipped another three blocks to the Dairy Queen, where she was meeting Beth. She came upon her cousin at the front of the building, reading the glossy advertisements for ice-cream cakes that were taped in the windows.

"Think we'll go to hell?" Beth said in greeting.

"Of course not, stupid," Danielle said.

Beth ordered an Oreo Brownie Earthquake and Danielle a cup of black coffee and a toothpick, and each enjoyed her selection as they made their plans for the rest of the day. The most pressing business was putting the final touches on their Halloween costumes. There were several parties that evening.

"I didn't look fat in mine, did I?" Danielle asked. "You can tell me if I did. I won't care. I'm thinking more about my arms, and maybe my thighs. Like, did the material cling to my—"

"Think we'll go to hell?" Beth interrupted. Her gum line was caked with Oreo crumbs.

"Listen—what we did last night was a good deed," Danielle said, twitching at the jaw; she had accidentally swallowed half the toothpick she had been gnawing on. "Lola Lundy requires psychiatric help and because of us she'll be getting that help."

Beth shoveled another bite into her mouth. "You can't fool me, Danielle. I know this is all about Brent Gaynor."

Danielle leaned against the vinyl seat and shook her head wearily, as if the effort of clarifying every situation for her blockhead cousin had simply become too much.

"Beth, think. Doesn't Brent Gaynor deserve better than a psycho for a girlfriend?" she said, gagging slightly on the wood splinters in her throat. "Mark my words, Beth. Someday I'll marry Brent Gaynor. I'll be Mrs. Danielle Gaynor. We'll live in Florida. In an A-frame cottage. On stilts."

"Yeah," Beth said, but she was thinking sadly about how the strokes of her plastic spoon had begun to reveal the bottom of her dish. "I guess."

Twenty-One

Someone was touching Lola on the forehead. She opened her eyes. It was Miss Bryant.

"You're very hot," the old lady said. "You have a fever."

Lola shivered. It was the opposite. She was cold. She noticed Miss Bryant was no longer wearing the pink pajamas but was dressed again in one of her shocking pantsuits.

"Is it morning?" Lola asked.

"You've been asleep a long time," Miss Bryant said. "All last night and all day. The sun's going down again."

Miss Bryant moved over to her kitchenette and ran a washcloth under the faucet. She put the cool cloth on Lola's forehead.

"You need a doctor," Miss Bryant said.

"No," Lola said. "It's just a little cold. A minor cold."

"It's more than that, I'm afraid," Miss Bryant said.

"But I can't go to the doctor," Lola said. "They'll put me back in the hospital. I'll be arrested. Arrested for the hundred dollars and for running away. I'll go to jail."

Miss Bryant sat down on the bed beside Lola. She had a thermometer and put it in Lola's mouth. "I know a few people over at the hospital," she said. "I'll go see them. Very discreetly."

Lola shook her head.

After a minute, Miss Bryant took the thermometer out of Lola's mouth and looked at it. "Not good," she announced. She moved over to the coat rack and took down her hat and coat. "I'll go now, and arrange things."

Lola knew it was useless to protest. Miss Bryant would not let her die of a fever in the projection booth. No civilized person could do that.

"All right," Lola said, and closed her eyes.

A moment later, when the front door slammed downstairs, Lola threw the blankets aside and stood up. Her head throbbed, but she couldn't worry about that. She had to leave. She'd find a better hiding place this time, somewhere nobody could find her— up in the woods at Eagle Rock or, if she couldn't make it that far, maybe in Fairview. All she needed was someplace where she could be alone to make a peaceful exit from this world. She thought of the Gadd brick factory, so conveniently abandoned and fenced in. She could scale the fence. She took a step toward the door of the projection booth and the blood seemed to drain from her head. For a second she couldn't see. She stuck out an arm and found the wall. *That's just from standing up too quickly*, she told herself.

She continued toward the door. She was doing all right now. She descended into the cluttered heart of the Yesterday Boutique. She had to get dressed. And quickly. The hospital was just two blocks away. Miss Bryant might be back within half an hour with the doctor, or twenty minutes, even.

She looked around. The choices were more than plentiful. She could be a sixties go-go dancer in a red rain slicker or a forties femme fatale in a strapless tulle ball gown. But she was tired and reached for the garment closest to her. It was a poodle skirt, but the zipper was broken.

She giggled. What was she doing anyway? It was ridiculous. These clothes were ridiculous. This was not her world. She dropped the skirt on the floor. She would not go to Eagle Rock after all, or scale the fence of a brick factory; she would go back where she belonged or die trying. She would not scurry around like a cockroach, like a rat, trying to avoid the police, Social Services, the hospital. This was beneath the dignity of the person she had become, the niece of Judge and Mrs. Wrigley, the beloved of Peter Hemmings. She would go home. And she would start immediately.

She went down the slope to the twenties rack and began sliding the hangers aside. The pickings were slimmer than she remembered. It occurred to Lola that she must have already taken the best clothes. Now she had to make do with the leftovers. She selected a faded lavender dress, a pair of shoes (from the 1940s, but it couldn't be helped), a rather moth-eaten fur coat, and a dilapidated, bell-shaped hat. She took off the nightshirt and changed into the vintage clothes right there next to the rack.

Then she climbed the stairs to the stage and exited into the wings. In a moment, the stage door banged behind her and she was back in the alley. It was dark and clear. The icy wind felt good to Lola. She set off in the direction of Ashfield High School, about two miles away. She avoided the main roads. Her bike rides had taught her various routes to the school, and she chose the one that passed through quiet residential streets with sidewalks. A person strolling along a sidewalk doesn't stick out, she thought, the way a pedestrian does on a busy highway. She was tired but no longer groggy or clumsy. She felt angry again, thinking about how they'd given her those drugs without her consent. But it was over now. It was all over.

She felt sure the portal would be open. She would go back, and she and Peter would marry—she was just the right age, wasn't she?—and get as far away from Ashfield as possible. They'd go to California, or New York, or take a steamer to Europe. And if she found the portal closed? No, she knew it would be open, expecting her.

She approached Ashfield High School. The wind blew twisters of grit and leaves around the courtyard. She was surprised to see lights on inside the school and the main doors standing open. She could have walked right in if she'd still had the key to the reserve room that Mrs. Dubois had given her. She had left it in her knap-sack, locked at the bottom of the chest in her big, lovely room at the Wrigleys'. Her mind ached trying to grasp where or when the key must be now. She would have to climb through the window. It wouldn't be easy, not with a bad cold coming on, not with a fever, she thought. But she could do it, and she would.

She noticed girls' voices behind her, giggling and laughing under the wind. She turned. At a distance of about fifty yards, in a swirl of leaves, she saw them. Whoopsie! Ruby! They stood near the gym doors in their long coats and cloche hats, their backs to her.

"Whoopsie!" she called out. "Ruby!" But her words flew off on the wind. The girls did not hear her. They did not turn. Lola walked toward them. The air seemed full of leaves now. The wind swirled around her like it wanted to swallow her up. It was hard to see. "Whoopsie! Ruby!" she called again.

At last they were only a few paces from her. She reached out and placed a hand on Ruby's shoulder. Ruby turned. But it was not Ruby. It was Danielle. The other girl turned—Beth. They were dressed as flappers from head to toe. Lola gasped. A wave of revulsion, of nausea, came over her. Now Lola noticed other fig-ures behind them, a pair of vampires, Darth Vader, Frankenstein, Spider-Man.

Halloween. She'd stumbled into the Ashfield High Halloween party. She took a step backward, and another. Danielle advanced and grabbed her hard by the sleeve.

"Lola!" she crowed over the wind. "We've been so worried about you."

"The whole town's looking for you," Beth began. "The police came, and Mrs. Hershey, and they—"

Danielle's scowl shut Beth up, and the big girl looked guiltily at the ground.

"It doesn't look like you have a date, Lola," Danielle said. "You ought to come with us. Come right this way with us. You don't look so good. Maybe you need help."

Lola yanked her sleeve from Danielle's grasp and ran, her destination the high window of the reserve room.

"I'll get Dr. Barton!" Danielle screamed at Beth. "You follow her. Don't let her get away! Run!"

Lola rounded the corner of the school, and the reserve room window was within reach. She felt faint now. Her lungs ached. The blood seemed to drain from her head as it had when she'd stood up in the projection booth. Her vision flickered on and off. She stood still for a moment until her eyes worked again, then climbed onto the low cement wall for the necessary boost. But the window seemed higher this time. The finger holds that she'd found easily before eluded her. She became aware of a commotion on the other side of campus, of voices, of shouting. The voices were growing louder, nearer. With all her might she heaved herself up.

Now she could see through the window. Neat bookshelves glowed, and the long leather couch, braced by reading lamps, stretched out against one wall. The wide oak desk held an inkwell. The pleasant smell of library books and floor wax filtered through the window. Lola shoved her arms through the opening and began to drag her torso through.

But something was wrong. She wasn't moving. Then she understood. Someone had taken hold of her legs and was pulling her back out. She began to scream, to beg to be released.

"It's all right, Lola. I've got you," came Dr. Barton's voice.

"No!" Lola screamed. "No! No! No!"

But Dr. Barton was stronger. He was winning. She was sliding backward. She grabbed the window frame as hard as she could, but the picture inside it was fading. The oak desk, the reading lamps, the glowing books, were vanishing like a mirage. In their place the green rubber garbage bin materialized, standing amid piles of rubbish. She felt herself fall into the arms of the man in the turtleneck sweater.

"It'll be all right now," Dr. Barton was saying in a low, soothing voice. Was he crying? Lola had the impression that he was. "We've got you. We've got you."

Lola looked around. A crowd had gathered. There were Incredible Hulks and Catwomen. And off to one side a pair of phony, treacherous flappers whispered to each other. A police car was just pulling up into the school parking lot. Lola could see its light spinning, but the siren was turned off.

Twenty-Two

Excerpt, Physician's report. Ashfield General Hospital. Oct. 31,
11:48 P.M.
Re: Lola Lundy, 16.

Admitted tonight in a highly agitated and delirious state. States
she is 17, although records check shows she just turned 16 in
June. Fever 102. Pneumonia confirmed by chest x-ray. Note:
Was arrested allegedly attempting to break into Ashfield High
School.

Excerpt, Nurse's report. Ashfield General Hospital. Nov. 3.
4:30 P.M.
Re: Lola Lundy, 16.
This girl has attempted to leave the hospital twice in the past
24 hours, although suffering from double pneumonia. Was
detained by an orderly both times. Would not explain her
actions. Psychiatric evaluation recommended. Note: Is a resi-
dent of Wrigley Group Home. Family history of major mental
illness.

Excerpt, Therapist's log. Hillside Psych. Wing, Nov. 15.
Re: Lola Lundy, 16.
Minor patient transferred here this morning from Ashfield
County Hospital where she was treated for pneumonia for
two weeks. Was scheduled to be released to Wrigley Group

*Home until evidence appeared via juvenile court that she had
set an arson fire at Ashfield High in September. Two cred-
ible witnesses made statements to this effect. Patient strongly
denies setting fire, and suggests witnesses conspired against her.
She is known to have committed a series of offenses, however,
including theft of a $100 from a fast-food restaurant, felony
car theft in another city (two years ago), as well as breaking
into Ashfield High at night more than once. She has also run
away from several foster facilities. Social Services sees an escala-
tion in the patient's anti-social behavior and believes her to be
potentially dangerous, particularly in light of her arson attack
at the school. Family has a history of major mental illness (i.e.,
schizophrenic mother, committed suicide approx. 10 yrs. ago).
Diagnosis pending.*

*Excerpt, Therapist's log. Hillside Psych. Wing, Nov. 21.
Re: Lola Lundy, 16.
Patient is withdrawn and depressed. Avoids eye contact. Refuses
to speak to any member of the staff, except to make statements
such as "I don't belong here. These people are crazy." Refuses to
participate in group activities or group or individual therapy.
Leaves her room for meals only but eats very little. Her clothes
were brought over from the Wrigley facility, but she refuses to
change out of the unusual vintage dress she was admitted in,
except for it to be washed. Dress is several sizes too large for her
and tattered. Will not explain her insistence on wearing dress.*

Lola's room at Hillside Manor was pale pink and rather small
with a window near the ceiling. She examined the window the
first moment she was left alone and found it maddeningly escape-
proof. The room had a poster of a bouquet of flowers on one
wall and a shelf with a few dozen books and magazines. For the
first few days, Lola lay in the bed and read, or just daydreamed.

She was no longer required to go to school. Therapists and nurses came in and out throughout the day, trying to cajole her into watching television with the crazies or joining in the handicrafts—handi-crap, she called it—or volleyball tournaments.

Nurses came and went with pills that Lola hid under her tongue and then spit out in the sink.

"You know what could cheer you up?" a nurse said one morning as snow came down outside the window. "You could write a letter of apology. Get things off your chest. You could be forgiven. Don't underestimate how good that might make you feel."

Lola looked up from her book, a beat-up paperback mystery. "Forgiven? For what?"

The woman smiled kindly. "I think you must know what. For the fire at the school, mainly. You could write to the school board and let them know you're sorry. It could be a first step toward your recovery. We could begin to get to the bottom of why you did it."

Lola felt like she was in a bad movie, the kind where somebody's been sent to the gulag without a fair trial. But she refused to be provoked. She turned back to her book. "There's nothing wrong with me," she said. "I didn't start a fire. I've never started a fire in my life."

"Have it your way," the nurse said. "I'll be in the multipurpose room if you have a change of heart." The nurse made a few other nonsensical remarks, and then, thankfully, left Lola alone.

Days went by. Lola watched the snow. One day seemed much like another, frozen and white. With time to rest, to reflect, to recover in the pink room, she could see the way time had twisted in on itself, how it could backtrack and jump forward. Time wasn't a straight line the way everybody thought it was. The fire department had listed the cause of the library fire as "unknown." They were stumped, naturally, Lola thought, because the answer lay beyond their time, undetectable. Peter had started the fire in 1924, but in the contortions of time, it had burned through the open portal in the reserve room to a few days *before* Mrs. Dubois had shown her the mess. The fire that Peter had set to keep her with him was the same fire that had brought her into the reserve room for clean-up duty, and had now flung them apart, a fire that had flickered between past, present, and future.

She replayed their last moments together over and over, trying to imagine what she could have done differently, but always came to the same dead end. How could she lament that Peter had set the fire? If he hadn't, she never would have met him, never have loved him at all. She felt the smallness, the weakness, of her mind. She imagined herself as a fish, unable to conceive of the world that existed above the ocean's surface.

At least they didn't take away my clothes, she thought. She stroked the lace neckline of the faded lavender dress as she stared up at the barred window.

A week later, Lola sat in the waiting room and stared at Dr. Schultz's pale yellow door. Soon she would see the doorknob turn and the doctor would appear, smile, and call her name. Lola dreaded the encounter, although it was she who had requested it. The time had come to explain her side of things once and for all, to present the facts, coldly and scientifically. It seemed a daring move, revealing all in a place where hallucinations were the rule, but it wasn't really, not when you considered that everything she was about to say, or nearly everything, could be backed up by history books, old maps, and newspapers that she could readily obtain.

Still, it wouldn't be easy to begin. She wouldn't be believed at first, but she was prepared for that. She would chip away at the doctor's doubts, the way a good lawyer does with a jury. She would describe events that took place in Ashfield, late 1923 and well into 1924, with all the rich detail that only a first-hand witness can provide. She would draw a layout of the town, complete with the old roadways and shops, forests and fields, cafes and dance halls, that hadn't existed in fifty years or more. She would name and describe dozens of townspeople. She would tell personal details about the Wrigleys, and about their home and servants. It could all be verified, or most of it.

The ward doors would slide open for her then, followed by the heavy doors to the outside world. She would run down the hill, across the frosty grass, and bum a ride, or catch a bus, straight to Ashfield High. The police would be called if anyone noticed her; she was an arsonist as far as the school was concerned. She might be able to slip past the metal detector without being noticed, but if that seemed too risky, she could climb in the window again. This time she'd make sure nobody was around.

"Lola?"

Dr. Schultz's door had opened and she was waving Lola in with the expected smile. Lola smiled back. She entered calmly, even gracefully, she thought, and took a seat on a floral love seat. The office was done in a palate of yellows, and a big glass coffee table sat in the middle, topped with a giant box of Kleenex and about a dozen vanilla-scented candles of various shapes. On one wall was a poster showing a hundred little cartoon faces, each one displaying a different emotion: happy, guilty, afraid, euphoric, jealous, depressed, and so on. A huge, glossy ficus plant stood in a pot off to her left.

"I'm glad you finally agreed to come in for a chat," Dr. Schultz said, settling onto a soft white chair across from Lola. "How's it going?" Dr. Schultz had long frizzy gray hair that she held back with a pair of rhinestone clips, and was partial to big colorful sweaters and jeans. Lola felt she was more open-minded than the other therapists in the ward, and had particularly asked for her.

"I feel fine," Lola said. "In fact, I don't think I belong here." She tried to look mild and ordinary. She folded her hands in her lap. Then she noticed the cloth-covered button that was dangling from a thread at her wrist. It occurred to her that maybe she should have taken off the flapper dress for this meeting and put her old jeans back on, and those stupid shoes they'd given her, sneakers without laces. It did seem kind of crazy to keep on wearing the dress. But somehow it was the principle of the thing. If she changed into her old clothes, wasn't it the ultimate act of surrender, an acceptance of this time and place where she didn't belong? Then again, she thought, she couldn't have changed even if she'd wanted to; they'd taken away her belt. The jeans wouldn't stay up without a belt. And clomping around with no shoelaces— if anything looked crazy, that did.

"Most of our clients feel they don't belong here at first," Dr. Schultz said. "Sometimes, for a young person, recognizing that something is wrong isn't so easy. But that's the thing that leads to recovery."

"But I'm not ill. I'm not," Lola said cheerfully.

"Uh-huh. Tell me more about that."

Lola noticed a beetle crawling on the ficus plant. She watched it for a moment, hoping it signaled good luck, and then looked back at the doctor.

"I'm sane. This isn't a place for sane people, is it? I'm not sure I can make it any clearer."

The beetle took wing. Lola turned her head slightly to watch it land on another leaf and wander around. She hoped her good luck charm wouldn't fly away.

"You've had problems, though. We'd like to help you tackle them, but you have to try, too."

Was this the right moment to tell? How should she start? Just blurt it out? Or sidle up to the matter, the way Whoopsie Whipple had sidled up to the punch bowl with her booze bottle?

"I do have problems," Lola ventured. "A lot of them right now. Just not the kind everybody thinks."

"How would you describe your problems?"

"They have to do with reality."

"Hmm. That's interesting. What about reality?"

"Reality and science," Lola said.

Dr. Schultz's mouth curled into a knowing smile and she began to nod. "Are you referring to the time-travel experience you talked about when you were admitted to the hospital?"

Lola was stunned. Had she already told them? "What did I say exactly?" she muttered.

Lola's unanswered question hung sickeningly between them. Dr. Schultz played with her pen and watched Lola closely. Lola turned her head to ward off the doctor's stare. She found herself looking at the plant again. She was sorry to see the lucky beetle spiral up into the air and disappear somewhere behind her.

"I think I understand why you wear that dress, Lola," the doctor said. "There's a very special secret reason, isn't there?"

Lola bit her lip and met the doctor's stare. She felt like she was seeing Dr. Schultz for the first time; her eyes were narrowed and yellow, her nose was long and sharp, and her gray hair seemed to bristle. She looked like a wolf. Her pen was poised on her clipboard, hungry for details, symptoms, any information that would confirm the diagnosis she had already made.

Lola clutched the arm of the love seat. She had been wrong about Dr. Schultz. She was not the right person to tell anything to. "I don't know what you mean," Lola stammered.

"I think you do, Lola," the doctor went on. "You told a story of traveling in time. I've been hoping to hear more about that—I mean, as soon as you were ready to share."

Lola began to laugh. She tried to make the laugh sound as merry as possible. She raised her eyebrows and fixed her face in a big, open-mouthed smile, taking a cue from the "amused" cartoon face on the poster. "I said *what?*"

"You said that you'd traveled in time. Through the reserve room in the school library. I've been wondering if these time travels might be connected to the fire you set, and to your dress. You ought to share all this with someone, get it all out and address it."

Lola laughed again, and this time, she couldn't stop.

"Do you mind telling me why that's so funny?" Dr. Schultz said.

"You think I meant it?" Lola asked.

"Didn't you?" the doctor said. "Don't you still?"

"Are you a real doctor?" Lola said. She knew it was rude. She meant it to be.

"Yes, I am."

"Then you should know a high fever can make a person delirious. I had a high fever, and pneumonia."

At that moment, the beetle returned. Out of the corner of her eye, Lola watched it fly in circles, land, and begin to explore a leaf.

Dr. Schultz tapped her pen against the desk. "Why do you wear that dress?"

Lola stood up. "It seems like proper attire for a nut house," she said. "But I can see I've been taken too seriously. I'm going to go and change. I would appreciate it if I could have my shoelaces back, at least."

"I'm afraid I can't do that."

Lola felt her blood heating and surging. She thought of Mr. Terry, a rotten perv in a stinking office. There seemed something honest about him now. He didn't try to mask his rottenness with vanilla-scented candles.

"I only came today because I have a request. I'd like to speak to my social worker, Mrs. Hershey. I have a right to contact her, don't I?"

Dr. Schultz nodded.

"Make the arrangements, then," Lola said, and in a second she was out the door.

Excerpt, Therapist's log. Hillside Psych. Wing, Dec. 4.

Lola Lundy, Case No. 1541-12.

Patient urgently requested appointment with me after being completely withdrawn and incommunicative since she was admitted here (Nov. 15). Demanded to be released. Says she is "sane" and does not belong in a "nut house."

Denies any memory of the delusions she reported when admitted to Ashfield General (Oct. 31). At that time, patient insisted that she had traveled through time via some secret path in the high school library. Now blames the fever that she was suffering at that time for her statements. Seems aware that she must convincingly recant these statements to secure her release.

Patient was aggressive, manipulative, hostile, and grandiose in her meeting with me today, and challenged my credentials. I suspect she believes that I am an "imposter" masquerading as a doctor, or suffers from another such delusion. She continues to wear the strange, vintage dress, unconcerned that it is stained and ripped. She appears to attribute some magical quality to the garment. In session today, I believe patient was suffering an auditory hallucination (hearing voices), possibly in conjunction with a visual hallucination, as her eyes continued to dart to her left side, as if she was taking direction from a figure or voice in that area of the room. Review of medications pending.

Note: A Miss Jean Bryant has telephoned reception repeatedly, attempting to speak with patient. Taking into account patient's delusional state, communication was denied, as this person is not a family member. Patient has requested to telephone her social worker. This is being arranged in accordance with state law.

Mrs. Hershey was sitting at her desk eating a cheese sandwich and doing paperwork when Lola's call came in. Lola wanted her to send over some books on local history, including a 1924 Ashfield High School yearbook. Mrs. Hershey had agreed.

She was glad to hear Lola sounding so normal. Had Lola ever sounded abnormal? She'd been rankled ever since Lola was committed to Hillside. It didn't seem right. But she told herself to face the facts, to remember the fire, and the break-in at the school on Halloween that had been seen by at least twenty-five witnesses.

Mrs. Hershey went to the public library after lunch, checked out a few history books, and put them in the mail to Hillside. The yearbook proved to be more of a problem. The oldest ones in the library dated from the late forties. Several copies were available in the state archives but couldn't be checked out, only viewed.

Mrs. Hershey felt sorry and guilty. She sensed she had somehow failed Lola, and was determined at least to find the old yearbook she wanted. That evening, at home, she checked a few auction websites and found a copy for sale in a small bookshop in another state. It was fifty dollars and reported to be in "acceptable" condition. Mrs. Hershey got out her credit card and ordered it. Delivery would take two to four weeks.

Although it was 10 p.m., she called Hillside. Anyone else would have been told to call back during business hours, but Mrs. Hershey had clout in that sad world of lost teens, and Lola was brought to the phone. She told her she'd mailed the history books but the yearbook would take a little longer. Lola seemed delighted with the news and thanked her.

Mrs. Hershey hung up the phone and sat down on the couch. She turned on the news but couldn't concentrate. She recalled what Danielle had said about Lola staring at an old yearbook for hours and hours. All she could think was: Why does she want that yearbook? Why?

Twenty-Three

Lola hung up the phone. She hated having to talk in the common room, which was full of loons who didn't know how to mind their own business. She had almost been asleep when she'd received the call from Hershey.

She walked back toward her room, noticing the light snow that had begun, and thought about Hershey's good news: Soon she would have the resources she needed to somehow build a case for her release.

She glanced about the large room. Most everyone was slumped in front of the television. Maybe that's why she noticed him, the young man in pajamas, off in a corner by himself. He was hunched over a table, working at something. She felt a sudden, overwhelming curiosity, and walked over to see what he was doing. With each step, her heartbeat quickened. She knew the set of the shoulders, the head of wavy brown hair, tilted a certain way in concentration, the hands that worked steadily, confidently. Peter.

Without a word, she pulled out a chair, sat down across the table from him, and waited for him to look up. But he did not acknowledge her arrival. He seemed not even to have noticed it. Lola saw that he was taking apart a telephone, an avocado-green push-button phone, twenty years old at least, the kind with the grating ring that could still sometimes be found in out-of date offices. She felt herself breaking out in a sweat in the chilly room.

"Peter," she whispered. "Peter. Look at me."

After a moment, he raised his face from his work, not to look at her but to choose a new tool from a small kit beside him on the table. Lola stared. It was Peter. But it wasn't Peter. His features had been somewhat rearranged and his green eyes were more hazel now. He was more like the brother of Peter, some strange, younger brother. But she felt not the slightest doubt. It was him.

"Peter," she said, more loudly than she'd meant to.

Peter did not look up, but Lola's voice drew the attention of several other patients and some of the staff. Soon a nurse had Lola by the arm and was pulling her down the hall. They veered into an office. The nurse shut the door. "Do you know this boy?" she asked.

"What difference does it make?" Lola said. After almost telling everything to the devious Dr. Schultz, she had swung the other direction and now made it a policy to reveal nothing.

"It's very important," the nurse said. "We have been trying to establish his identity. He won't speak to anyone. We'd like to know who he is, so we can locate his family. He's been here for a month now, and it would help if—"

"A month?" Lola said. "What day did he get here?"

"Do you know him or not?" the nurse said.

"What day?" Lola insisted.

"It was sometime around Halloween, I think. Maybe just before."

Lola understood now, why Peter hadn't come out of the reserve room after setting the fire. At that moment he had fallen through. And now they were both here, imprisoned.

"He was found wandering in the parking lot of Rite Aid, near the high school," the nurse was saying. "But the high school people don't know him. If you know anything, Lola, we'd like you to—"

"I've never seen him before," Lola said.

She went straight back to the recreation room. Peter was gone. She felt desperate, and furious at the nurse for pulling her away, but there was nothing she could do. She had to stay calm.

"Lights out," one of the staff was saying. The TV watchers had turned off their program and were meandering away to take their medicines and go to bed.

Lola was awake all night. She had to talk to Peter. She tried to think of a way to sneak into his room, but the boys' sleeping area was on the other side of two sets of locked doors that could be opened only with a keycard. She would have to wait until morning to see him again. For now she was left with the frightening image of him, so silent and so changed.

What had happened to him? He had come through the portal, but something had gone wrong. He hadn't remained intact. He was ghostly, airy, mute, a rearranged person, like a puzzle put back together the wrong way. It wasn't surprising; she had always felt changed for the better in Peter's time, a brighter version of herself.

She remembered a spring day in Peter's workshop. She had been strumming the ukulele and fumbling with his science questions. *I know what you're thinking*, she had told him. *You're thinking, of all the future girls, why did you end up with one who doesn't know anything about science?*

And how had he answered? *If you hadn't come to me, I would have found you. Somehow I would have.* Lola sat up and watched the snow through the little window. One thing was certain: It was her responsibility to take Peter back to where he belonged, to make him whole again. But how? She worked on the problem until the sky got light. Then she went to the common room to find him. She wore the lavender dress. Something from his era, she thought, might make him feel more at home.

Peter was seated at the same table as the day before. The phone was in front of him, reassembled. He opened his little tool kit, removed a screwdriver, and set to work, taking it apart again.

"That's all he does."

Lola turned. It was another patient. A girl with neon-pink hair who was always in trouble for stealing things. Marsha? Melinda? She couldn't remember. She hadn't bothered to make any friends.

"Huh?" Lola said.

"That guy. He takes that phone apart every morning, and puts it back together every afternoon. Haven't you noticed?"

"No," Lola said. She took a step toward Peter.

"You're not going over there, are you?"

Lola ignored her and took another step.

"He never says a word to anybody. They think maybe he never learned to talk," the girl went on. "What a freak."

"Shut up," Lola said.

The girl gave her a dirty look and walked away.

Peter was bent over the table, just as he had been the day before. Lola pulled out a chair and sat down across from him, and again, he showed no sign of noticing her.

"Peter," she said. "I wish you'd talk to me."

She watched his hands, which were something like Peter's but not quite, remove the plastic casing from the phone and set it aside. The inner workings of the push buttons were exposed.

"Won't you even look at me?" she pleaded.

But he did not.

Lola sat with Peter all day, except for the meal breaks, watching him dismantle the phone down to its tiniest components and then methodically reassemble it. His complete unawareness of her made her feel like a hovering spirit desperate to communicate with the living.

She wished she had the yearbook. When it came in the mail she would slide it in front of Peter. He'd be forced to look at it. Maybe then he'd be stirred from his trance.

Days passed and Lola kept her vigil across the table from Peter. The Hillside staff noticed her sudden, baffling interest in the silent boy, and questioned her about it. She was summoned into the wolf lair—her new name for Dr. Schultz's office—and reported that she enjoyed watching him take the phone apart and put it back together again.

The holidays arrived and Lola was urged to join in decorating the recreation room and trimming the tree. Volunteers were being sought for a caroling group that would stroll Wings A, B, and C on Christmas Eve, spreading cheer. It was too sad to be funny. She told them to go away.

Therapist's log. Hillside Psych. Wing, Dec. 12.
Re: Lola Lundy, Case No. 1541-12.
Patient depressed and antisocial. Rebuffs invitations to group activities, sports, crafts, as well as therapy. Has developed a strong interest in another patient (case no. 07-515) whom she sits with for hours every day in Common Area B-4. Situation so far neutral but closely monitored.

After a week or so of watching Peter in silence, Lola began to talk to him. In a low murmur that nobody else could hear, she spoke of people they both knew: Thumbtack, Whoopsie, the Wrigleys, Virgil, Ruby, Miss Roach. She talked about the picnics at Eagle Rock, dances in the gym, afternoons of swimming, and the long, blissful hours they'd spent in Peter's workshop.

"Do you remember the reserve room?" she said one day. She had been leading up to the question. "Do you remember what happened there? What happened to you and me?"

He did not answer but paused for a second or two before continuing his work on the telephone. She was sure, then, that he had been listening, and that the mention of the reserve room had struck a chord. She felt a thrill, and continued more boldly.

"We have to get out of here," she whispered.

Lola then began in earnest to think up a plan. She would have to steal a keycard from one of the nurses. They clipped their cards to their belts, or hung them on straps around their necks. The belts were the easiest targets. She'd wait for a commotion—there were several minor riots every week, usually stemming from a disagreement over the television channel—and seize the opportunity to unclip the keycard. Then, sometime deep in the night, she would make her escape with Peter. They would run down the hill to the employee parking lot. If nobody was around, Lola could hotwire one of the cars on the spot. If it seemed risky, they could walk for a while before trying again somewhere else.

Alone in her room, she rigged up a simulation, using a playing card attached by a hair clip to the sleeve of one of her shirts. She practiced stumbling, bumping up against the sleeve, and the quick pinch of thumb and forefinger that would release the card. After several dozen practice runs, she thought she could do it without being detected.

On a weekday in mid-December, Lola woke up and looked out her window. The sky was a bright, shocking blue. It gave her courage. Today was the day she would tell Peter the plan. He might not respond, but she knew he would listen. She had noticed the way his pupils sometimes dilated when she spoke, or how a foot would start to tap. She was convinced that he listened to everything she said, and would follow her instructions.

She put on her vintage dress, and feeling free already, entered the common room. Her eyes went straight to the corner table where Peter always sat. But he was not there. She looked around and then she saw him, sitting on the couch in the corner next to a middle-aged woman, a visitor. She was holding his hand, and he was talking to her. He was talking! An overnight bag sat next to him on the couch. Dr. Schultz sat in a chair across from them, nodding and smiling.

Lola approached them. She was confused and afraid. What did they want with Peter? What were they doing to him? Near the couch, she stopped. The woman visitor looked up, and then Dr. Schultz did.

"Peter?" Lola said.

Dr. Schultz stood and touched Lola's arm. "This is Brian Snyder, Lola, and his mother, Mrs. Snyder, from Harrisburg, Pennsylvania."

Lola was too shocked to move. "He can talk?" she said.

Mrs. Snyder put her arm around her son. "Brian has a rare form of autism, combined with a condition called selective mutism," she said. "He does talk, but only to certain people. There are only four or five people he will speak to."

Brian turned toward his mother. "That's the girl I told you all about. The girl who thinks she's a time traveler. She thinks I'm one, too. She's so crazy."

Brian's voice was high and raspy, like a rusty spring, nothing remotely like Peter's. A terrible, desperate anger filled her. She wanted to grab this imposter by the throat and shake him. This was not Peter Hemmings. How could she ever, ever, in a million years, have thought so?

His face wasn't the right shape at all. He was shorter than Peter, and his hair was straight. Her mind had made him into Peter. Her mind had done it all. Only her mind! She turned to run, but Dr. Schultz had her by the arm. She wrenched away and heard the rip as the entire sleeve came off her lavender dress at the shoulder. She fled, but the un-Peter's high, weird giggle followed her, rising above the other sounds in the room.

Twenty-Four

In the days that followed, Lola spent hours and hours in the yellow therapy room. Dr. Schultz already knew her secrets; she had learned them from Mrs. Snyder of Harrisburg, Pennsylvania. Brian Snyder had a superior memory, common to people with his disorder, and he had told his mother verbatim every single story that Lola had whispered across the table.

Dr. Schultz was fascinated by Lola's case, and dove into it. She was writing a paper on Lola for the next state conference; it would be ideal, the doctor thought, if Lola could make some significant strides in her therapy before the paper's deadline in the spring. The report would have all the more impact then, and might even generate interest from a book publisher.

Lola could not fight anymore. She put on the old jeans without a belt and the sneakers without laces. She threw the rag of a dress into the trash and took the medicine she was given. She could not deny that she had believed with all her might that Brian Snyder was Peter Hemmings. And if she could believe that, how much else of what she'd experienced had been a hallucination? Like crazy people everywhere, she'd been convinced of her sanity.

The doctor had tried to help Lola see how it had happened: It was the strain, she'd said, the terrible strain of returning to Ashfield, the place where her mother had died. Emotions long submerged had caused her to yearn for her home again, but home was gone and she had reached into her imagination for a replacement.

"It's an understandable reaction," Dr. Schultz said one afternoon a week after Brian Snyder's departure. "But escaping into fantasy isn't a positive reaction to stress. It might feel good while it's happening, like drugs or alcohol, but in the end it's pulling you further and further away from a healthy life."

Dr. Schultz offered Lola a piece of hard candy in a bowl shaped like Santa's sleigh. Lola took one and played with the wrapper but didn't eat it. It had begun to snow again, and the psychologist's window was a square of pure white, like a blank slate. Lola was marveling again at the power of her own fantasy but was pestered by all the things she'd seen in the past that were verifiably real.

"But Peter Hemmings was a real person," she said. "And so was Whoopsie Whipple, and Thumbtack and Virgil. They're all in the yearbook. They're all real."

"We keep coming back to that, don't we?" Dr. Schultz said. She got up from the sofa and wandered around the room, stopping to pluck a couple of dead leaves from her ficus tree. "The county might have their birth and death certificates. We might be able to find something out about who they were. It could help you to see how different the real people were from the fictional characters you created from the portraits."

Lola toyed some more with the candy. She felt as if her head wasn't attached to her body. She'd often felt that way since she started on her regimen of medications.

"What about my cap? My cap was on the chair," she began.

"An object was on the chair," the doctor corrected, then sat down at her computer and hit a few keys. "I've been looking over your story in a lot of detail, Lola, and a number of interesting things jump out at me."

"Like what?" Lola said dully.

"You said that when you first met Peter, you felt you'd seen him before, that strong jaw, that wavy hair. You recognized him because you had seen him before, in the yearbook. You added the voice, gave him a personality."

"But I'd barely skimmed through the yearbook then. I couldn't have recognized him."

"There's so much we unconsciously see, take in, without realizing it. We focus on the objectives of our daily lives: the traffic light that tells us to stop, the store clerk who's asking us for a credit card, a ringing telephone. But everything else in the background does register on us. Our subconscious collects everything and uses it. We think dreams, fantasies, ideas, come from some other dimension, some magical place, some special inspiration, but they come from material that has all been put before us, the scraps of our lives and feelings."

"If I can overlook that much information, then I'm the least observant person in the whole world," Lola said. She unwrapped the candy and sucked on it. It tasted disappointingly of herbs.

"You found that strange compartment in the library with the glass bottle, and then the first thing that happens in your time-traveling world is that the girl finds something in the little compartment, right?"

"Yes," Lola admitted.

"And then, when she talks to you by the punch bowl, what's the first thing she asks you?"

"I forget."

Dr. Schultz scrolled down the long report.

"She asks you if you are a member of the Temperance League. And one of the books you'd just been reading before you fell asleep, wasn't it an old book about temperance?"

"I think it was," Lola said.

"Your quick scan of the yearbook told you what the front of the school looked like in 1924. It told you that the mermaid fountain once had a head. It told you what the band looked like, how the gym was decorated, how the students dressed."

Lola thought of the mermaid. She wished they'd get it over with and tear her down instead of just leaving her there year after year, decapitated.

"You didn't leave the school with Peter that night. Do you know why?"

"I went back to get my knapsack."

"No. You couldn't leave with Peter, because you didn't have the information to do so. You didn't know what stood outside the school. You didn't have the ingredients to make that world, to create the streets of the town, the cars and houses. Not until you met Jean Bryant and looked at her books."

"Miss Bryant was nice to me."

"Only *after* Miss Bryant showed you that book about the Wrigleys did you begin to imagine that you went to the Wrigleys' home. Your bedroom there was an idealized version of the room you shared with Danielle Anderson. Right down to the same tree."

Dr. Schultz had criticized Miss Bryant all week long. In her estimation, the old crackpot had left Lola alone with pneumonia in a drafty attic, and encouraged her mental breakdown with talk about invisible audiences and holes in the skin of time.

"She told you about a champion pole-sitter, brought down by bad weather."

"Mr. Bill Penfield," Lola mumbled.

"And then what happens? You imagine a friend, atop a pole, brought down by bad weather."

"Struck by lightning. She fell from the top," Lola said, "but survived."

"Impossible, see? And think about this: The only 1920s film you had ever heard of was the one playing when you went on your date."

"*The Sheik*," Lola interrupted. "Valentino."

"You understand now that it wasn't a coincidence. Not at all. You saw what you knew about."

"But—"

The doctor looked up. "Yes?"

"How come I know what happens in that movie?"

"You'd seen it."

"No. I'd never seen a silent movie."

"You did. When you were too little to remember. But the subconscious never forgets."

Lola's head had floated even farther away than usual, and seemed to be hovering somewhere over her left shoulder. Her eyes felt heavy. She wanted to sleep.

"I guess you're right," she said.

Twenty-Five

The medicine made Lola drowsy and stupid. But it also brought on a kind of numbness that could almost pass for peace. The struggle she'd waged was over. Now that she'd gone crazy like her mother, she didn't have to worry about everybody waiting for her to do so. She only had to take the medicine and follow the routine laid out for her by Dr. Schultz and the nurses. It wasn't hard to do what they asked, to shuffle from one activity to the next in her laceless shoes.

Lola climbed the stepladder to place the star atop the Christmas tree, and on Christmas Eve she joined the other carolers—she no longer called them "nuts"—to tour the other wings, spreading cheer.

They strolled first through Wing C, the disabled wing. Nurse McDonald led the carolers, dressed in a Santa hat and giddily playing the role of an orchestra conductor; she was new to Hillside, young, and still enthusiastic about her job, the picture of efficiency with her crisp white smock and neat blonde hair.

Lola was pleased that the group's performance had brought smiles to a few faces. It was a good thing she was doing, a sane, real, kind thing. Her job was to carry a basket of candy canes but make sure not to give them to anyone at risk of choking.

Dark had fallen by the time the carolers arrived at Wing A. Some of the old people smiled at the carolers, some cried a little, perhaps remembering other Christmases when they were still able to participate in life, and a few of the more lucid ones sang along.

"Great job, group," the nurse-conductor sang out, brimming with Christmas cheer. "We're gonna be heading back now, but let's make a special stop here to see Mrs. Ryan. She didn't feel much like leaving her room tonight, but she's a very special lady—one hundred and four years old last month."

Mrs. Ryan was propped up in her bed and opened her eyes when the carolers entered in full song: *Jingle bells, Jingle bells, Jingle all the way.*

Mrs. Ryan was like a tiny white bird, Lola thought, with her cottony tuft of hair standing straight up on her head. She watched the carolers, but her neutral expression did not change; it was hard to tell how much she was taking in. The room was small and stuffy, and Lola found herself smashed up against the wall under the television.

"Merry Christmas, Mrs. Ryan," Nurse McDonald shouted as the performance concluded. Mrs. Ryan seemed to nod slightly, and then closed her eyes. In the disorganized exit that followed, a stray elbow knocked Lola's basket of miniature candy canes and they shot out in all directions on the slick hospital room floor. The carolers dove for them, creating a sudden chaos that the nurse hurried to quell.

"Everybody up off the floor, please," she sang, clapping her hands. Marsha, the pink-haired kleptomaniac, was stuffing two handfuls down her pants. "Lola, you go ahead and pick up the candy canes and rejoin us in the multipurpose room. Everybody else, time for cocoa and cookies."

A shout of delight went up from the carolers as they stampeded toward their reward. Lola set about her task. Some of the candy canes had slid under the bed, and she saw several stuck under a radiator.

As she crawled around the floor, filling her wicker basket, Lola noticed that the old lady, who a moment ago had appeared to be asleep, was watching her. She leaned forward and craned her crinkled neck, showing far more interest in this janitorial task than she had in the caroling performance.

"Hello," Lola said, unnerved by the staring.

Mrs. Ryan made no answer but brought out an old, old hand from under her bedspread and picked up a pair of heavy glasses from the bedside table. She put the glasses on and looked at Lola.

"Am I dead?" she croaked.

Lola stood up in surprise. She had assumed Mrs. Ryan was long past talking.

"Have I gone to heaven?" the old lady demanded.

Lola glanced out the door for a nurse, but the corridor was empty. Everyone was at the party.

"No," Lola said. "This isn't heaven."

The old lady put her head to one side and stared even harder at Lola. "Then why are you still young, Mike? Why are you still young and I'm so damn old?"

Now Lola recognized beyond a doubt the tone of the voice, the blue of the eyes, the shape of the face. The basket fell from her hand. Her heart was beating out of her chest. *I'm not crazy,* was all she could think. *I'm not crazy. I was never crazy. They made me think I was crazy, but I never was.* "Whoopsie?" she said.

"Ha. Nobody's called me that in eighty years," the old woman said.

Nurse MacDonald's loud, honking voice could be heard from over in the multipurpose room, directing the festivities. It seemed that at least for the moment, she had forgotten about Lola and the spilled candy canes. Lola pulled the door closed and grabbed Whoopsie's hand.

"It is you. It is."

"Yeah, it's me all right," Whoopsie said. "Or what's left of me."

"I can't believe it. Look at you. You're so old," Lola said. "You're ancient."

"I know," Whoopsie said.

"Did you dance on Broadway, like you wanted to?"

"Oh yes. In the *Follies*."

"What else? Did you get married?"

"Six times. Saw the pyramids. Sailed down the Ganges on a barge. The whole nine yards."

"Everything you wanted."

Whoopsie blinked under her glasses and her chin trembled a little. "But none of it any good without Thumbtack. I never spent a truly happy day after I lost Thumbtack."

"You never went back to him?"

Old Whoopsie pinched the corner of her bedspread and drew it up to her eyes. She was crying. "I couldn't."

"Couldn't? Why not?"

"Don't you know, Mike? Didn't you hear? Thumbtack came to look for me. That summer I left. He ran his car off the road halfway to New York and was killed. It was the thirtieth of August, 1924, at four o'clock in the afternoon."

"No," Lola said. "It can't be." Then she remembered the hot day at the swimming hole, when Thumbtack had been so restless. He was already thinking of going to get Whoopsie.

"I wanted to come home for his funeral, but they wouldn't have me. The town wouldn't have me anymore. Not even Mother and Daddy. They wouldn't see me. They all said I'd killed Thumbtack with my flightiness."

Lola put her arm around Whoopsie's shoulder. Whoopsie felt boneless under her thick robe, like nothing more than a pile of soft clothes.

"So I went on with the chorus line. That first one. I forget the name."

"The All-Cutie." It was fresh to Lola, as fresh as last month.

"Yes, I believe that was it. I left that operation after a month or two. That impresario wanted more than dancing out of us chorus girls, if you get my meaning. He was a dirty old rascal. Fink was his name and it fit. Wouldn't even give me my back pay when I quit. I couldn't go home, so I just joined up with another outfit, and another, and oh, I don't know how many others. The years kept on rolling; one marriage, then another. I came back to Ashfield when I was eighty-one, after the last people who remembered about me were gone. I looked after myself until I was ninety-six, and then the old carcass gave out and I ended up here—people bringing me Jell-O all day and singing at me. We used to come here and sing at people. Remember that?" The old lady shook with a few silent sobs. Then she seemed to think of something and looked up toward the door. "Is Peter with you? Is he young, too?"

"No." Lola said. "He isn't here."

Whoopsie looked down at her hands. "Oh yes, I remember now. I'm sorry, Mike. I'm so sorry."

"Sorry?" Lola felt a cold trickle of dread. "About what?"

"Peter. You loved him."

"Something happened to him," Lola said. The words felt like poison in her mouth.

"Don't you know? That fire. At the school. He died in the fire. Oh, such a long, long time ago. People said he'd set it himself. Set it because you'd disappeared and his heart was broken."

"No. It isn't true. It didn't happen."

"A terrible thing. The dear professor." Whoopsie gazed up at a point on the ceiling. "How come you don't know? Have you lost your memory? I've still got mine and sometimes I wish I didn't."

"I have to go back to him. Tonight," Lola said. "I'll change what happened."

"Are you an angel?"

"No. I just know a way to go back. I'll go back, and I'll stand in the way of it."

"For Thumbtack, too?"

"For both of them."

A wave of laughter came from the party in the next room and snow skittered on the window, as if someone had thrown a handful of rice at the glass.

Whoopsie closed her eyes, and for a moment Lola worried that she had dozed off. But when she opened her eyes again they were bright and alert. "Imagine. If I could see Luther again, one more time, only for a minute—I could sit on a park bench and wait for him to pass by. He wouldn't notice me, an old, old lady on a bench."

Whoopsie's hand found the top of her head and scratched. "He wouldn't know me now, of course. Not without my curls. Not with these false teeth." She chomped her dentures up and down. "You sure I'm not dead?"

"I'm sure."

"You're the one who's still young, so you must be the one who's dead. You're a ghost. Right?"

"Nobody's dead."

"I don't get it, Mike, but take me back with you if you know how," Whoopsie said. "I wanna see Thumbtack before I croak."

Lola held Whoopsie's relic of a hand. It was out of the question, wasn't it? Whoopsie was outlandishly old, *Guinness-Book-of-World-Records* old, or almost. "You look pretty delicate, Whoopsie," she said. "The trip might be hard."

"What? Afraid I'll die?" The old woman clutched at her blanket, and with a grunt pushed it aside, revealing her two matchstick legs, blue with veins, that ended in big red bed socks. "Come on, Mike, take me along. I'm all ready to go."

Lola felt she had no right to deny the request. Whoopsie only wanted what she wanted: to go back and see the person she loved.

"Can you walk?" Lola said.

"Not too well. I've got that wheelchair."

Lola scooped Whoopsie up from the mattress and set her down in the wheelchair that was standing behind her bed. She was nearly as light as the wicker basket of candy canes. Lola pulled the blanket from the bed and began to tuck it around her legs.

"Hold on there," Whoopsie said. "Hold on a minute." The faded blue eyes looked back at Lola. They were confused, dreamy, as if part of Whoopsie had already gone to the next world.

Lola knelt down beside the wheelchair. "Change your mind?"

"Hell, no. I forgot to put on my lipstick." Whoopsie patted Lola's arm to let her know it was a joke, and for a second Lola recognized the girl in the pink dress and the long beads who'd sipped hooch in the reserve room.

She pushed the wheelchair to the doorway and set the brake. "I'll be right back."

Twenty-Six

The party had not ebbed, and in fact Nurse McDonald was putting on a new CD as Lola closed in on her. Lola's eyes were fixed on the nurse's back, with its starched white smock billowing out on both sides, and dangling from the right pocket, her key-card badge.

Speed, Lola told herself. *Do it fast.*

She moved into position behind the nurse. Around her everyone was laughing at a joke someone had just told, and the gongs and sleigh bells of Christmas were pouring from the CD player. No one was looking. With a quick flick of thumb and forefinger she sent Nurse McDonald's Santa hat sailing toward the floor. As the nurse bent over to retrieve it, Lola unclipped the badge from the pocket of the white smock and it dropped into her hand.

Lola turned and began to retrace her steps. Twenty paces away she allowed herself a backward glance. The party was continuing as if nothing had happened. One of the girls had launched into a funny anecdote, and the others had crowded around to listen. Nurse McDonald was choosing a cookie. And then she noticed Marsha. From the center of the crowd Marsha was watching her with a kind of secret surprise written on her face, her plastic cup of cocoa halted halfway to her open mouth. She had seen.

Lola quickened her pace back toward Whoopsie. She wanted to run but didn't dare; every orderly in the place would appear if she started to run. She stepped into Whoopsie's room, grabbed hold of the handles of the wheelchair, kicked up the brake lock, and pushed toward the exit.

The first obstacle was the nurse's station. Lola made small talk as they rolled past, pointing out the Christmas decorations, and Whoopsie nodded along, as if they were out for a pleasant sight-seeing trip through the ward. One nurse sat behind the desk, staring at the computer. She glanced up at the pair as they passed her station and said nothing. The security doors came into view but were still far off at the end of the long hallway. The wheelchair skimmed past a series of patient rooms. Over the jabbering of televisions someone was moaning at perfect two-second intervals. The woeful sound made Lola itch to run. She and Whoopsie were twenty yards from the locked doors, then ten, then five. Lola readied the key-card badge. In that instant it entered her mind that the card might only open the doors in the youth psychiatric ward where Nurse McDonald worked, but as she swept it through the slot, a green light appeared. Lola shoved open the door. They were free.

She pushed the wheelchair through the set of doors, and then through another unlocked set that led to the outside. The cold, clean air hit her like a slap as she angled the wheelchair down a ramp. She paused to pick up a heavy piece of sandstone near the front doors that was left over from a summer rock garden, and continued down the long path toward the parking lot.

The snow, heavy now, dimmed the lights overhead. Lola was grateful for the cover as she threaded along the rows of parked cars.

"Which one's yours?" Whoopsie asked.

"We're stealing one," Lola said.

"Stealing?"

Lola stopped beside a beat-up Ford Taurus and raised the rock to smash the driver's side window.

"Wait," Whoopsie said. "Don't."

Lola turned back. The old lady had extracted one of her arms from under the blanket and was pointing with a trembling finger at a vintage Cadillac parked next to them. "That one's better."

Lola turned away from the Taurus and heaved the rock through the Cadillac's window, reached in, and snapped the door locks open. Then she lifted Whoopsie from the wheelchair and buckled her into the front passenger seat. The next challenge would be finding a flat-head screwdriver. Lola tore through the glove compartment and then the trunk, but there was nothing. Despite the cold, she was sweating. She glanced toward the building she'd just left. *What if I'm caught?* she began to think, but suppressed the idea. There was no way but forward, and no time to entertain thoughts of failure. She raised the rock and smashed the passenger-side window of the Taurus. Inside the glove compartment she found a wallet containing $50 and some credit cards. She dropped the useless wallet on the seat and popped the trunk. She could have screamed with joy when she saw the heavy plastic case marked "Craftsman."

By the trunk's weak light she found the screwdriver and the bonus hammer she was hoping for, quietly closed the trunk, turned away from the Taurus, and flung herself into the Cadillac's driver's seat. The flat-head fit neatly into the key slot. Lola pounded the handle of the screwdriver as hard as she could with the hammer to break the ignition cylinder. *One turn and it should start,* she thought.

"I think they're onto us," Whoopsie said.

Lola looked up. A posse of orderlies was pouring from Hillside's front doors. They ran toward the parking lot. Marsha. Pink-haired Marsha. She'd told.

Lola twisted the screwdriver and the big engine roared to life. She backed the car out normally, just in case there was any hope she could pass for a staff member leaving after a shift. At this, the orderlies began to sprint toward the car, but they were too late.

Lola steered out of the parking lot and onto Hillside Boulevard, heading straight for Ashfield High School.

The drive was only five miles, but after half that distance Lola heard multiple sirens. The thickening snow made everything fuzzy. Lola was afraid she might crash. It was like nightmares she'd had where she was barreling down the highway but her eyes would only open a slit.

Lola pressed down on the big gas pedal and veered into an alley, a shortcut she knew from her bike rides, as Whoopsie hunkered in the seat. In a minute Ashfield High appeared, half-hidden under a curtain of falling snow. Lola drove into the parking lot. The sirens were louder now, and seemed to be circling, getting closer and closer, like wolves. Time was running out. Lola slammed on the accelerator and with a cry of "Hold on, Whoopsie!" piloted the big Caddy across the school parking lot and straight through the chain-link fence that surrounded the school. Snow and turf flew as the car rounded the campus, dragging a mangled fence panel, and pulled up right under the reserve room window.

Lola flung open the car door, and grasping the hammer jumped up on the low wall to the reserve room. She felt sick when she saw that the window had been boarded over with several wooden planks. In two seconds she was back behind the wheel, circling the building, hunting for another point of entry. And then it hit her. Why not the main entrance? *It's our school. We'll walk right in the front door. Right in through the front like anybody else.* She stopped the car and rushed up the steps with the hammer. There were double glass panels on both sides of the door and she went to work on them, smashing again and again. With each hammer blow, the sirens seemed to grow louder. The police were behind the school. Avoiding the jagged edges, Lola finessed herself through the window frame and into the dark interior. She leaned on the long push-bars across the middle of the doors and they banged open. Frozen air blasted over the threshold, carrying snow. Lola could hear voices, faint but urgent, on the wind. The police appeared to be on foot now, coming across the campus. Lola dragged the wheelchair out of the car and shoved it open. When she turned again, she saw that Whoopsie had managed to open the car door a few inches and had stuck one of her pitiful legs out. Lola lifted the ancient lady from the car and placed her in the wheelchair. She forced the wheels through a stretch of snowy ground and started up the concrete ramp to the door. The ramp was slick with ice and the chair skidded sideways. Lola's half-frozen fingers cramped over the handles. There was no traction. She backed down the ramp and tried again. This time the chair flew over the ice, and in two seconds was at the top. Lola looked over her shoulder as she pushed the wheelchair into the school. The silhouette of a man had appeared against the field of white, and as she watched, several more men materialized. A whole posse was jogging toward her with searchlights, eight or nine people at least. She doubted they could see her yet, or even the car. They must have been following the tracks.

She pulled the heavy front doors shut and heard the click that meant they had locked behind her. She took off running, past the metal detector and the payphone and the long banks of dented lockers, past the principal's office and under a team-spirit banner. Somewhere behind her she could hear a kind of banging at the doors she'd just shut. The police couldn't get them open, and the officers were too big to get through the hole in the glass. Lola herself had barely fit. But she was sure they would find a way in. The question was, how long would it take? How long did she need?

Lola ran faster and now her chest burned. One of her shoes, lacking its laces, flew off. She pulled off the other one and her socks, too, and kept on running toward the library. Her feet slapped on the cold floor as they had the night of the dance. She'd never run so fast. The walls seemed to blur with the speed. Lola turned a corner and came to the library door. She tried the handle.

It was locked. She would have to smash the glass in the door, and realized with horror that she'd dropped the hammer at the main entrance. She looked around for something else she could use, then thought of the fire extinguisher that was kept a little farther down the hall. She ran for it. In seconds she was back, lugging the heavy red tank. She moved Whoopsie out of harm's way and heaved the extinguisher. The crash was loud, and glass flew. Lola stuck her arm through and opened the door. At the same time she became aware of lights bouncing along the walls. The men with the searchlights were in the building now, and close.

Lola wheeled Whoopsie into the library and smelled burning. She looked toward the reserve room. The door was ajar and smoke spilled from the gap.

"It's through there," Lola said.

Whoopsie coughed and peered into the smoke. "That's the way back?"

"Yes," Lola said.

"I want to walk now," Whoopsie said. "Help me up."

Lola took Whoopsie by the arm and felt her rise to her feet with a kind of superhuman last effort. Whoopsie took a step, but there was no force left in her. The legs buckled. Lola lost her grip as the old woman stumbled forward into the dark room.

"Whoopsie!" Lola screamed, starting blindly after her friend. The room was full of smoke and shadows. Lola's groping hands found a bookshelf, then a wall. Where was Whoopsie? She pivoted around. Her foot touched something on the floor. It was a body. She dropped to her knees.

And then she saw him, lying unconscious by the long sofa.

"Peter!"

She grasped him under the arms. He was a dead weight, too heavy for her. Then she felt someone lifting Peter's legs. She looked up. Through the smoke she saw Whoopsie, dressed in an old lady's nightgown blackened with soot and two sizes too small for her.

Lola was stunned. The trip had stripped most of a century from Whoopsie's odometer. She would not be the old, old lady on the park bench after all.

"I got my end," Whoopsie said. "Ready?"

Together they carried Peter out of the room, out of the library, back out of the school, and into the hot summer night.

Peter's car was still waiting where Lola had last seen it, getaway style, in the alley. And then she heard his voice, weak but clear.

"Put me down, girls."

Whoopsie dropped the legs and Lola lowered the top half. Peter landed in the grass with a sneeze.

"What happened?" he asked.

Lola didn't answer but leaned down and kissed him over and over, and he kissed her back.

"Don't kiss. Breathe," Whoopsie ordered, pushing her brown curls back from her sweaty brow. "Lola, can't you see the man's all oven-roasted and hickory-smoked?"

Lola collapsed onto the grass beside Peter, her hands still frozen but sweating with the August heat, her lungs expelling fumes and frost. Whoopsie sat down, too. She pulled off the big red bed socks and flung them off over the lawn.

"I always hated these damn things," she said.

"Are you wearing a nightgown?" Peter asked Whoopsie. "And when did you get back from New York?"

"A lot happened while you were unconscious," Lola said.

"A century, professor," Whoopsie added.

Peter sat up. "I've got to write this down," he said, patting the pocket of his vest. "Where's my notebook?"

Rising over the chirp of the crickets came the thin wail of a solitary siren. The volunteer fire engine was on the way. The three teens scrambled up from the ground and made for the car.

Whoopsie got there first and slid in behind the wheel. "It's my turn to drive. First stop's Thumbtack's house," she said, and pressed the button labeled *START*.

ASHFIELD DAILY HERALD

ASHFIELD - (Dec. 25) Police are seeking a female mental patient who is believed to have removed an elderly woman from the Hillside Manor health facility last night.

Lola Lundy, 16, took advantage of a lapse in security during a Christmas party to escape the facility, police said. It is unclear whether Ryan went willingly with Lundy or was abducted. A spokesman at Hillside said Lundy has a history of mental instability and a criminal record that includes burglary, arson, and grand theft auto.

A review of close-circuit footage allegedly showed Lundy hot-wiring a car in Hillside's employee parking lot, although Saturday night's blizzard obscured the images, police said. The car was later found abandoned on the lawn of Ashfield High School with its doors hanging open.

A window at the front of the school had been smashed with a hammer that was found at the scene. Tracks suggested the two women had entered the school, but they were not found inside after a thorough search, police said. Several wheelchairs were found in the school on Sunday, but it was not immediately clear if any of them belonged to Ryan.

"We are confident that we will find Miss Lundy and Mrs. Ryan in the next twenty-four hours," Police Chief Lucas Smith said Sunday. It will be very difficult for Miss Lundy to remain at large with Mrs. Ryan for any significant length of time."

The stolen car was a 1977 Cadillac DeVjnille registered to Vivian Schultz, a psychologist employed by the Hillside facility. The car sustained major damage, police said.

Twenty-Seven

Miss Bryant was used to getting crank telephone calls. The worst were the ones in which you answered the phone only to be addressed by a robot who wanted to sell you life insurance or inform you you'd won a sweepstakes you hadn't won at all. So when a "Mr. P.R. Donaldson, attorney-at-law" telephoned two days after Christmas with his "exciting news," she was not inclined to believe it. "Is this a real person talking?" Miss Bryant said.

"Yes," the voice said. "As I indicated, I'm P.R. Donaldson, attorney-at-law."

"And you say I've won a house?"

"Not won. Inherited."

"Somebody left me a house, you say?"

"A Dr. and Mrs. Hemmings of Palo Alto, California."

Miss Bryant sat down on her celery crate and scratched her wig. She could not remember anybody by that name. She did not believe she knew a soul in Palo Alto. And yet, it stood to reason that she knew these people. Otherwise, why in the world had they left her a house?

"Are you still there?" Donaldson said.

"Yes, I'm here. Is it a historical home?"

"As a matter of fact, yes," Donaldson said.

"They've left it to the society, I believe you mean to say, to the Ashfield Historical Society, of which I am the current president."

"No," Donaldson said. "To you. To you personally. You are Miss Jean Bryant?"

219

"Yes. But I'm not sure I can accept an entire house from some people in California I never met. It's a bit strange, wouldn't you agree?"

"Do you at least want to come and look at it?" Donaldson asked. "Then we can move forward from there."

That afternoon, Miss Bryant found herself riding in Mr. Donaldson's car to an old neighborhood near the high school. The day was bright but clear, and the sun sparkled on the high snowdrifts that hemmed in all the roads of town. Mr. Donaldson's radio crackled softly with Christmas music. They passed the high school and continued down the block. Mr. Donaldson turned onto Elm Street and stopped at Maple.

"Here it is," Donaldson said, jerking up the emergency brake.

Miss Bryant looked at the turn-of-the-century cottage, white, neat, and framed by pines. Donaldson guided her up the icy walk. It did not take long for them to tour the six empty rooms. Mr. Donaldson mentioned a sort of a shed, or small barn, that was part of the property.

When they finished, he pulled an envelope from his briefcase and handed it to Miss Bryant.

"This came with the bequest," he said.

Miss Bryant opened the envelope. It was a portrait of a young couple. *Brown Portrait Studios, San Francisco*, it read, and it was stamped May, 1938. Miss Bryant put on her glasses and the blurry faces came into focus. By gum, if it wasn't Lola Lundy. So she'd done it. She'd seen that train passing on the parallel track and she'd jumped.

Miss Bryant turned back toward the lawyer.

"It's a charming little house," she said. "I believe I have just the right period furnishings for it."

"So you do want it?" Donaldson said, looking up in surprise from some documents he'd been organizing. "I figured you'd want to sell it. I could arrange that for you."

"Oh no," Miss Bryant said. "I shall live right here."

Epilogue

Mrs. Hershey hadn't even packed up, and a guy in overalls was already scraping her name off the door with an X-Acto knife. She had taken all her files out of the cabinets. The old ones were destined for the shredder. The newer cases would all be computerized. The department was cutting down on paper and improving efficiency. But she wouldn't be around to see it.

She bent down to clear a stack of files out of the lowest cabinet. She flipped through, and the names on the files brought faces into her mind that she had not seen for a long time. Danielle Anderson. Yes, the skinny girl. She'd be almost thirty now, if she hadn't starved to death. She'd married some basketball player and gone south. The boy's name wouldn't come to her. Brett? Bart? Buddy? She flipped to the next file. Jared Fantino. Twenty-five to life for first-degree murder. She fed it into the shredder and picked up the next one. Sienna Martin—a porn actress, last she'd heard.

She set aside the stack and leaned over again to make sure the file drawer was cleared. But no, something was still there, a package, caught in the drawer runners. She yanked at a corner and out it flew, throwing her off balance. She found herself seated on the floor with the package in her lap. It was from a bookstore, addressed to her, but unopened.

Then she remembered: It was something she'd bought for Lola Lundy, that book Lola had wanted so much, all those years ago at Hillside. It had come in the mail a few weeks after Lola's disappearance.

Lola. They'd never found her. Or the old woman. Where was Lola now? In jail in another state, more than likely, or maybe not even alive anymore. Mrs. Hershey felt sad and heavy there on the floor and wondered if she had done anybody any good at all in her entire life. She tore open the package. Yes, she'd been correct: There it was, *ASHFIELD HIGH: 1924.*

She paged through, trying to imagine what it contained that had so captivated Lola. She smiled at the stiff-collared staff of Ashfield, and the billowing bloomers on the girls' basketball team. She read the students' outdated names, listed in a column beside the class photographs: *Edith, Hershel, Mabel*—she'd had a great-aunt Mabel herself—*Ruby, Edna, Virgil.* She came to the junior class. *Lucille, Clarence, Thelma, Herbert, Lola. Lola Lundy.* Mrs. Hershey took in a breath. She adjusted her glasses and looked again: No, she hadn't been mistaken. It did say "Lola Lundy." Her eyes sought out the photo that went with the name. A terrible confusion came over her as she found the picture. It was Lola. It was Lola Lundy, the girl she had known, suspended in an oval frame, smiling at her in shades of gray.

She got up from the floor, shoved the junior class page featuring names from H to M under her desk lamp, and, for a good ten minutes, stared at it: Lola Lundy. Without a doubt, that *was* Lola Lundy. It was, but it couldn't be. She had the same feeling of uneasy skepticism that came over her whenever she saw a card trick or a magician. There was an explanation. She just wasn't seeing it.

She sat down in her chair, took a bite of her burrito, and chewed, listening to the scrape, scrape, scrape of the workman's blade, which had now pared down her name to "HE." After a minute she began to laugh softly to herself. A coincidence, that's all it was. Lundy was a common enough name, and so was Lola. There had probably been other people named Lola Lundy over the decades. Now she knew why Lola had wanted the yearbook: She had liked that picture of the girl who shared her name. Maybe the girl had even been a relative, a great-great-grandmother or aunt, and Lola had found comfort in looking at the picture.

Still, the card-trick feeling hadn't gone away. What about the stunning likeness? And that smile? She drummed her fingers on the old book and thought. Could it be, possibly, that she no longer quite remembered what Lola Lundy had looked like? Could the old photograph have fused itself to the fragment of Lola in her memory? She had seen so many teenage girls come and go, so many, many, many. It was a wonder, really, that she could picture any one of them clearly. She slipped the yearbook into her purse to take home. Then she stood up and turned back to her files. It was late, and there was still so much to do.